Allison shivered in her wet arm... pelted her face and scalp. Her long hair clumped at the nape of her neck and each cold drip that slithered down her back felt like the icy fingers of death tracing her spine. She huddled in the bushes, conscious of how her armor chaffed her skin despite its fine craftsmanship. At least, she reflected, she wasn't alone in her misery. As she looked to either side of her, she was faintly satisfied to see that her friends were as miserable as she. Well, all of them but Jimmy. Like the others, he had pulled his cloak close, but not for warmth so much as to hide the glint of the mail vest he wore over a light leather jerkin. The last weeks had seen him not only grow in size but also take on more of the traits of his native northland people. Fifty degrees and raining was a warm summer day as far as he was concerned. The mail had come from the Bonecrushers—the goblin tribe they had helped—and wasn't exactly sized for his bulk. Nevertheless, he'd managed to squeeze into it anyway. It was a good thing he had, too. It had saved his life at least once since he'd donned it. Allison wondered, not for the first time, why she wasn't as at home in the cold as he. The back story she'd made up included her character being Jimmy's best friend's sister and she had grown up in the same icy northern hamlet. Perhaps her sensitivity to the cold had something to do with the fact that she remembered none of that shared history.

Stu held his enchanted bow close to his body to protect its ... he Kobold co... ned some we... little rain wa... habit—at least it seemed like years to him now—weren't so easy to dismiss. His other hand remained empty, ready to draw an arrow or perhaps the short sword at his side in case it came to melee. He preferred to plink away at enemies but had long since gotten used to things not going as he preferred. He unconsciously rubbed the knot on his head where he'd been clubbed by kobolds, and shifted his weight anxiously from foot to foot, both nervous tics that he no longer seemed to notice. The young woodsman didn't like cities and was eager to get back out to nature. A surprising state of affairs, Allison reflected, for the son of two doctors and younger brother of ballerinas.

Chuck huddled down in the shadows, his cloak pulled tightly around him, hood up. He was completely still—she couldn't even see him breathing. In fact, the only reason she could see him at all was because she knew he was there. In contrast to Stu, it was clear that the little rogue was in his element here in the city, alternating between a bravo's swagger and a cutpurse's inconspicuousness as the situation required. Although he had left the back alleys and criminal gangs in his past (not his real past, she had to remind herself), he hadn't lost any of his skill or street savvy. She knew that beneath his cloak he had a dagger ready to throw and had already scoped out at least two ways of escaping if things went awry. Once she would have called that cowardice, but that was before he risked everything to save them from the ogre Crackrock's lair. Now she just thought of it as a knack for survival.

Of the four boys with whom Allison had begun her journey—five, she reminded herself, thinking briefly of their fallen friend Simon—it seemed that TJ had changed most of all. She turned her gaze toward him, only to find him staring back, as if he had been expecting her look at just that moment. He gave her a nod and a reassuring wink, then turned back to his watch. Rather than changing physically, like Jimmy (or to a certain extent Chuck), TJ had changed in what she could only describe as *stature.* Each day he seemed less the carefree teenager that had begun the adventure and more like a wizened wielder of arcane might. Maybe it was the feeling of magic flowing through him, or maybe it was the accumulated knowledge of his magical studies crashing into his memories and blocking what had been there before. Whatever the cause, he seemed less her friend and more her companion.

Allison wondered whether the others saw the same sorts of changes in her. She didn't really think she was any different than she used to be. She knew, however, it might look that way to her only because she was growing more into her character and remembered less of how she used to be. That was one of the things that pushed her to keep going and to find a way back home. While her newly gained powers were impressive and, she had to admit, sometimes fun, she liked being a teenager people weren't trying to kill on a regular basis, and really wanted to play *that* character again.

So, the five waited patiently in the dark, cold rain. Each thinking their own thoughts, each wondering what the future would bring.

A light flashed in the darkness, followed by the sound of footsteps beating a hasty retreat down the road. Chuck whispered, "That's our sign." As one, they dashed across the street and entered an alleyway piled high with boxes and refuse. A small path, wide enough for only a single person, had been cleared through the mess. In the dim light of the street lantern behind them the five could just make out the faint outline of a stairway leading into the sewer below. Each of the friends took one last gulp of clean air, steeled their resolve, and descended into the unknown.

MORE FUN AND GAMES

DAVE BARRETT

This is a work of fiction. Names, characters, organizations, places, events, and incidents are either products of the author's imagination or are used fictitiously.

Edited by Alyssa Archer

http://www.alyssaarcher.com/

Cover Design by Karen Lucky

https://www.facebook.com/luckykarenart/

ISBN 978-0-578-21461-0

e-ISBN 978-0-578-21462-7

For Danielle, Andrew, and Christopher.

No, really. I actually wrote it for you.

TABLE OF CONTENTS

THE STORY THUS FAR...

After years of pestering, high schooler Allison Duggan finally agrees to join her best friend TJ's wizard character on a weekend-long live action role playing adventure. The pair are joined by veteran gamers Stu, an archer and woodsman; Chuck, a rogue with a dark past; Jimmy, a barbarian from the North; and the least likely participant, Simon, the starting tailback for TJ's and Allison's high school football team, who shows up painted entirely blue. Allison is quickly assigned the role of party healer, and the group sets off on a quest on behalf of their king: travel to Estervary and destroy an evil wizard bent on ruling the world.

Not long after an ominous meeting with a goblin character, the group notices odd occurrences, from surprisingly detailed props—including sheep and young children—to open prejudice toward Stu's dark skin, to their having knowledge and memories in their heads that weren't there before. The truth that they had somehow crossed over into their game world comes crashing down upon them when an all-too-real arrow shot by an all-too-real bandit kills Simon.

Resolving to continue their mission in the hopes of finding their way back home, the friends are captured by a group of brutal kobolds acting on behalf of Crackrock the ogre, one of the wizard's minions in the west. As part of a daring escape orchestrated by Chuck, the group befriends a goblin wizard and make their way to his home, the Bonecrusher clan's mountain fort.

PROLOGUE

Magnus was on his throne, looking down at one of his many servants. He reflected on the fact that he was spending far more time on his throne than he used to. Such was the cost of power, he mused. The more he conquered, the less time he had for conquering. At least it was a nice throne, gleaming of gold and platinum, and bedecked with jewels of all manner. Its armrests were in the shape of tigers crouching to pounce, and its back was an eagle, wings spread wide. The servant before him looked almost identical to the last, and to the one before. They were like ants scurrying about here and there, always with great purpose but never with any noticeable outcome.

"Oh, Greatness," the man began with a bow, the cuffs of his long sleeves dragging against the floor. "The emissary from Providence City has arrived as commanded and is waiting outside for his audience with you. Would you like me to bring him in?"

The wizard sighed. Speaking of ants, this emissary's

hill was large and could be a problem. Not something to cause a halt to his plans, but it was an annoyance he didn't want. Even worse, the barbarians who had taken up residence near the city were unpredictable and quick to insult. They would all need to be properly managed. "Yes, show him in, and then you are dismissed for the day. He will be able to show himself out."

A flash of worry danced across the servant's face. Dismissal from the wizard's presence was sometimes more than a simple dismissal. His predecessor had discovered that after doing nothing more than bringing unfavorable news. Others learned that lesson for no discernable reason other than the wizard's moods. It seemed as though he treated his followers as mere playthings to be discarded on a whim. The servant backed away quickly, head bowed in reverence, while Magnus smiled at him benevolently.

Moments after the servant left, a new figure strode purposefully through the throne room's wide doors. This newcomer was dressed in riding leathers dusty from the long trip. The clothes were well made and stylish, sporting the stylized leaf motifs currently in fashion in the west, and were tailored to show off the man's broad shoulders and trim waist. The emissary himself had washed his face and hands before entering, and droplets of water glistened in his well-trimmed goatee. Between the dusty clothes and the wet face, he looked almost like a cow fresh from the water trough. Thirty feet from the dais upon which the wizard's throne sat, the man stopped, doffed his hat, and bowed low.

"Oh Great Wizard of the Arcanum. I, a humble representative of Providence City, have come to attend you as requested. I have traveled hard and fast and we are eager to learn your will."

Magnus chuckled. The man before him was many things, but humble was not one of them. Be that as it may, there was work to be done and such trivialities were unimportant. He leaned forward in his throne and began, "Thank you for coming on such short notice. I appreciate your and your masters' diligence." The man's eyebrows twitched slightly at the mention of having masters, much to the wizard's delight. This one had ambition. "I understand that your nation has been plagued by a host of wild men and women. Indeed, as I understand it, they have settled right on your doorstep. I imagine that your people are troubled by this outcome?"

The man smirked disdainfully and nodded. "Filthy creatures all. Would that we could eliminate them, or at least drive them off. Alas, we do not yet have the might, though perhaps with your aid we would find victory. In fact, many in our government would be quick to bend the knee to you out of gratitude."

"Is that so?" Magnus pondered the situation. He didn't need an alliance with Providence City to achieve his goals. They were, in truth, irrelevant to everything. And yet tools deemed worthless at one juncture could well be useful at another. He smiled. "I am not yet ready to march my armies west in force. However, I believe I may have an alternative solution for you, one that will, if not cripple them, cause such a rift in their society that they will cripple themselves." The emissary leaned his head forward conspiratorially as well. "There is in their possession an artifact of great power …"

CHAPTER 1

The friends emerged from the goblin's dining commons for the last time and found themselves bathed in warm sunlight. Birds sang to each other cheerfully, and a low buzz floated in on the breeze from the direction of the town's apiary. After escaping from the dwarven fortress in which Crackrock and his followers had set up camp, they had made a beeline for the wizard Eggelbert's home, the home of the Bonecrusher clan. Of the six (including Eggelbert himself), only Chuck had come out reasonably unscathed from the ordeal. As it happened, Allison's powers were better at healing life-threatening wounds than fixing up aches, pains, and the effects of being manhandled cross-country and chained for days in a dank cell. The friends had made the most of Goblin hospitality, staying several long weeks before finally feeling ready to press on toward the East and their quest.

Goblin men and women went about their business, some hanging laundry from the second floor balconies of their squat buildings and others heading off to start their days as blacksmiths, weavers, and the like. Goblin children ran underfoot, having long since let go of their anxiety about the humans staying in their town. Older ones strutted about, copying either Jimmy's bold strides or Stu's more graceful gait. Carved into the face of the cliff around which the town had been built, the tribe's deities looked down upon them all. Some smiled and some frowned, individual personalities etched according to some long-dead sculptor's whim. Their traveling gear lay neatly placed near the town's well. It was time to go.

Finkelbert, the tribe's chieftain, approached the friends, a sad smile upon his face. During their visit he had spent quite a bit of time in their company, sometimes brainstorming with TJ about how to get home and how they had gotten to this world in the first place, sometimes just playing host to heroes that had literally saved his tribe from certain destruction. He was going to miss not only their company but also their protection. With their new allies, Clan Bonecrusher would be no easy nut to crack. The chief knew, however, that the humans' destiny was not to live their lives out among his tribe of goblins.

"So, friends," he began, "it is now the time for travel, and the time for farewells. The Bonecrushers are sad to see you go, but we wish you the best of luck!" At this, the goblins who had wandered over to see what their chief was up to burst into a cheer. This subsequently drew more goblins over, who began cheering as well, and it was some time before quiet was restored. Chief Finkelbert seemed unperturbed by the outburst; he bobbed his head and smiled, as if he had expected it all along. Perhaps he had.

When the gathered throng quieted, he motioned to the side and Eggelbert approached the group with arms laden, many of the items in them glinting in the sunlight.

"Brought what you asked of me, I have," Eggelbert said to the chief, giving him a slight bow. Though he was the most powerful wizard in the tribe, and was married to the Chief's sister, he acted in public like any other member of the Bonecrusher clan. He spoke in the human tongue for the sake of the five, none of whom could understand the goblin's own grunting language. Like most of the clan, his command of the common tongue of the humans was imperfect, and the friends often shared smiles over his vocal similarities to Yoda, the Jedi Master. The chief nodded his thanks and returned his attention to his guests.

"The service you have performed for us, both in helping rid us of the kobold menace and in returning our Egg to us, is truly great, and I and my kin have expressed our gratitude to you on more than a few occasions." There was a smattering of applause at this, but the irritated glance he gave to the crowd silenced it much more quickly this time. "We now will express our gratitude in a more tangible manner. At the beginning of your quest I promised you shinies if you came to our aid. I think you will find our gifts shiny, indeed!" Turning back to Eggelbert, he reached out and took five small purses that hung by their drawstrings from his brother-in-law's thumb. He handed one to each of the friends saying, "Our hills, and therefore our clan, are not rich in gold. Despite that, I believe these should see you well provisioned for your journey." While the others all tucked the purses into their belts, Chuck hefted the pouch, trying to gauge its weight and listening for the clink of coins. Not hearing much beyond a dull clacking, he loosened the drawstring and tipped the purse over into his hand, despite the stern glare he received from Allison. It wasn't gold and silver coins that spilled out, but gems, both cut and raw. A grin stretched across his face, and when he looked back at Finkelbert he saw a twinkle in the goblin's eye that mirrored the light refracting through the stones in his hand. Not rich in gold, but the wealth contained in any single one of those bags would have been enough to set them up comfortably for the rest of their lives.

"While the contents of those pouches will keep you fed and sheltered, we also have gifts for you that will keep you alive!" Draped over Eggelbert's arm was a shirt of shining metal rings, forged together so tightly that it looked more like cloth than armor. Despite its apparent bulk, the chief easily lifted it and held it at arms' length to appraise it. After looking back and forth between the shirt and Jimmy several times, he finally nodded his head and declared, "That ought to fit." In a softer voice, he added, "more or less." He handed it to the large man, who was looking at it somewhat askance.

"You sure about that?" Jimmy looked doubtful that it would fit over his shoulders.

Chief Finkelbert bobbed his head and said with a grin, "More or less!"

Shrugging, Jimmy slipped his arms through the shirt, then raised them to let gravity do the work of pulling the mail over his shoulders. Just as the little goblin had predicted, it did indeed fit, more or less. Jimmy moved his arms up and down and twisted his torso back and forth several times to assess what the armor would do to his freedom of movement. He then stepped back a few paces, drew his massive sword from its sheath, and proceeded to go through a series of thrusts, cuts, and parries as the assembled goblins looked on. The sunlight glinted off the hundreds of tiny facets of the mail, making the plaza look as if it were hosting a disco. He slid the sword back into its sheath, slung it across his back, and nodded his approval before stepping back to where the group was standing. "Thanks a ton. This is pretty slick." Finkelbert raised an eyebrow at Jimmy's choice of words, then shrugged and turned to pick up the next gift.

Addressing Stu, the chief said, "An archer, I think, could use different tools." Taking a set of silver bracers from Eggelbert, he stepped forward and strapped them to Stu's forearms. The metal was intricately worked with images of men hunting a large stag, firing arrows as they chased the animal through the woods. It seemed to Stu almost as if the figures were moving and the arrows actually flying across the metal, though never quite reaching their fleeing target. Aside from the obvious protection the metal plates provided, he could tell that his already considerable skills with bow and arrow were magically enhanced to superhuman levels. Between the bracers and the enchanted bow, it was likely he would never meet an archer his equal. With an embarrassed blush, he gave an awkward bow in thanks.

Finkelbert then handed a pair of scuffed looking boots to Alison and smiled as he said, "I've heard that you aren't exactly the quietest member of your group when walking in the woods. These ought to help with that." Allison blushed at the boys' snickers and took the offered gift, immediately sitting down to take off her old shoes. She slipped the new ones on and laced them all the way up, past her calves. Although the black leather was old and beaten up, the boots felt soft and snug on her feet and the laces held tight. Allison stood up and tentatively took a few steps. She didn't feel any different, but then the Bonecrushers' main plaza wasn't really the best place to experiment. If they did work as advertised, though, she knew this was a wonderful gift. Of the five, she was the least experienced and the only one whose character hadn't taken points in the Woodcraft skill. Even TJ, the bookish wizard, could move quietly when he needed to. She scooped Finkelbert up and gave him a big, squeezy hug, followed by a kiss on the top of his head, to both his surprise and his delight. "Thank you so much," she exclaimed after putting him back down.

The chief then presented TJ with a golden ring set with a large ruby. Around the central stone were half a dozen diamonds. Four shone brilliantly, each worth a small fortune by itself, and two had a smoky appearance. The Chief gave no explanation, glancing first at Eggelbert and then at the human expectantly. TJ turned the ring over in his fingers, several times squinting at this or that aspect of it as he went through the massive catalog of lore that had flooded his mind over the past weeks. After a few minutes, he looked up at the Chief with a raised eyebrow and said, "Az'karnor?" Finkelbert grinned and Eggelbert actually clapped his hands in delight.

"Told you he would know, I did," the younger Goblin crowed.

TJ slipped the ring on his finger and said with a bow, "Thank you, this is a fine gift. I have read more than once about these rings, and I never expected one to be hidden away here among your people!"

"Hidden away, it was not," Eggelbert said, and wiggled the fingers on his left hand. "Told you, I did. Great and powerful wizard, I am. Travelled many years, I did. Slew great monsters, I did. Great treasures, I found. Found this out, Crackrock did!" He let out a giggle and pointed a finger at TJ with a *pshew* noise.

TJ laughed at this and replied, "Crackrock surely did discover how great and powerful a wizard you truly are! Thank you for giving me this ring. I would refuse, but I think I will need its power before our job is done. Instead, I will treat it as a loan, to return to you when next we meet."

The two goblins exchanged a glance and Chief said, "We also look forward to the day that you will return to us," though he sounded less than optimistic. After a reflective pause, his face brightened back up and he said, "And now, we wish you the best of luck. This is only the beginning of your journey. May the rest of it be quick, safe, and successful!" The assembled goblins again let out a cheer and then dispersed to attend to their daily activities.

Looking around in confusion, Allison said in a stage whisper, "What about Chuck? Didn't you forget him?"

Chief Finkelbert blushed slightly and he glanced toward Chuck, who broke the awkward silence by saying, "Oh, you know me. A big bag of jewels and stuff? That's more than enough!" He flashed a grin and added, "And anyway, if you remember, I'm the one who saved all of *your* bacons. You're the ones who need the extra help, not me.

As far as I'm concerned, we're all square, the Bonecrushers and me." Finkelbert looked visibly relieved.

"OK, if you say so, Chuckles." Allison didn't look convinced.

"I do," he replied ending the discussion.

What the others didn't know was that he had already received his gift from the tribe. The day before, when the rest of the group was out and about mingling or exercising or doing whatever, the Chief had taken him deeper into the mountain's tunnels than he had ever before visited—or even realized existed. Eventually they arrived at a small room filled with alchemical equipment. Steam rose from bubbling beakers set over charcoal braziers, and a goblin Chuck didn't recognize was hunched over a table, extracting a clear fluid from a series of glass vials connected by tubes. Chuck and Finkelbert waited patiently in silence, not wishing to disturb what could be a dangerous process. After several minutes, the goblin looked up with a grin. He hopped off his stool and strode toward them, holding a small vial of the fluid in his hand.

Chuck raised an eyebrow in inquiry, and the goblin said simply, "Watch." He unstoppered the vial, dipped a pin into it, then reached into a cage where a small, chinchilla-like creature huddled. Taking the squirming animal in his hand, he pricked it lightly with the pin and placed it on the ground. The creature, sensing freedom, took two rapid hops toward the exit before collapsing with a twitch and going still.

Chuck observed, "That's a nice display, though I feel sorry for the little guy. He was kinda cute. I'm not quite sure why you brought me to see that," he said with a shrug, before continuing. "There have got to be easier ways to rid yourself of vermin than going around poking them with needles."

"You're not fooling anyone," replied Finkelbert with a dismissive wave of his hand. "You know very well how useful such a concoction can be." Chuck remembered the crow—Eggelbert's wizard familiar—that had led him to where his friends had been held. To gain entrance to the kobold fort (and rescue his friends) he had to rely on the skills he had learned as a guild-trained assassin. He had hoped to keep that part of his history a secret, but the crow had obviously reported what it had seen, and Chuck mentally slapped his head for not having thought of it before. Oops.

With a sigh, Chuck countered, "OK. Even so, why are you showing it to *me*?" He picked up the creature and gave it a quick glance before saying, "It's not like I don't have options that do that already. Maybe it's a little faster than what I currently use, but not much."

"Because," the unnamed goblin said as he gently returned the ball of fur to its cage, "yesterday, full of a deadly poison that one was." He gestured at a second cage, where another floppy eared furry thing was munching away happily at some carrot greens. The alchemist had apparently studied the Human tongue with Eggelbert,

"No way," Chuck said, reaching into the cage to retrieve the still creature. He inspected it closely, checking for any signs of life. There was no heartbeat. No breathing. Its eyes had dilated. It was well and truly dead.

"Way," the Chief assured.

"That...that is truly amazing." His mind raced, thinking of potential uses. He looked up. "How long?"

"Depends on the dose, according to our friend here." The nameless goblin bobbed his head, happy to turn the discussion back over to someone with a better grasp of the language. "As few as fifteen minutes, as long as four days. That one should be awake within two hours or so." He nodded at the ball of fluff in Chuck's hands.

Chuck replaced the dead-yet-not-dead animal and took the offered vial from the alchemist's hand with newfound respect. He mentally calculated how many human doses he could get out of it: not that many. "Thank you very much. I am grateful." After a moment he added, "Any chance you'll tell me how you made it?"

The two goblins exchanged a quick glance before Chief Finkelbert said, "Nope."

With a good-natured grin, Chuck replied, "Didn't think so, but figured I'd ask. I'll take good care of this." He gave the vial a little shake before tucking it into a pocket on his vest. The two retreated through the tunnels and then parted ways, the Chief headed to do chiefly things, and Chuck to put his prize away in the special case reserved for those sorts of tools.

So, while Chuck had already gotten his thank you gift, it wasn't something he was particularly interested in sharing with the rest of the group. Rather, he was happy to keep quiet about it and pretend that the money he'd received was all the reward he needed. Maybe it would have been easier to share his secret skills with his friends, but the cautious nature of his new persona made him hold it back for the time being.

The goblins had no horses other than the gigantic draft horses built more for pulling plows than carrying people, so the friends set off on foot. This suited all of them but Stu and Jimmy anyway, since the two were the only ones with any experience riding a horse. Back in the real world they had all read enough stories about erstwhile heroes riding horses for the first time and then having trouble walking for a week. When they reached the palisade gate, they all turned around for one last look before leaving.

"Wow, total déjà vu feeling right now, isn't it?" Allison remarked. It hadn't seemed that long ago since they had set out from another camp, off to do battle with the great foozle to the east. Of course, before, it had just been a game. And before, there had been six of them instead of only five. The others murmured their agreement and they all turned and walked into the rising sun, wondering what was in store for them next.

CHAPTER 2

The friends traveled east. Secluded as they were, the goblins didn't have a lot of information about the threat coming from Estervary. All they knew was that the wizard-king who had bested his fellows in the Arcanum had turned his eyes westward, though that was hardly news to the friends. It was, in fact the reason that they had begun their quest in the first place.

"Estervary is hundreds of miles away," Allison commented as they walked across a wide field of calf-length grasses spotted with vibrantly colored flowers and the occasional shrub. "What was he doing with Crackrock this far west? I thought we'd have a lot farther to travel before we started running into any of his forces. Shouldn't we be worried about that?"

"Good point, Allie." Jimmy replied. "It's one thing to encounter random monsters…"

"Like those wolf men back in the real world?"

"Exactly," he agreed. "Those are absolutely normal in

this sort of adventure. But running into what amounts to a boss monster this soon? That never happens. Magnus has moved west far faster than we expected."

Chuck nodded his head thoughtfully, but TJ spoke up. "Well you are assuming that we are still even inside a 'game.' I don't know about you, but I gave up on the whole game thing right around the time that Simon died." He fell silent for a few seconds, lost in memories, before continuing, "But look on the bright side. At least Magnus isn't exerting his power directly. So long as he continues to need minions like Crackrock it means he hasn't completely established his grip on power. There may still be a chance for us to defeat him. Let us at least take heart in that."

After only a short distance, the heroes came upon a cobblestone road running east-west. While it seemed to have been originally designed to be wide enough for two carts to pass, over time stones on the edges had come loose or been stolen. In its current state of repair, a single cart driven down the middle had no more than a foot of buffer on either side. At some point in the past, the trees within thirty or forty feet to either side had been cut to increase visibility and protect travelers from ambush. Since then, shrubs, ferns, and even some small trees had slowly begun to creep back toward it. Despite its shortcomings, this was a far cry from tromping through the woods and the five were grateful for it.

Once again, the five set the marching order with Stu in front and Jimmy behind, the three "squishies" protected by the beef. Part of Allison took offense at her inclusion in the category of squishy—she had her steel breastplate, after all—and she had to remind herself that compared to the others, she wasn't exactly "muscle." She had limited weapon skills, felt awkward in her armor at times, and because her character was brand new, couldn't take nearly the damage that any of the boys could.

At nightfall they set up camp just off the side of the road. After going through the trauma of being clubbed and captured by kobolds, they decided to take turns at watch rather than trusting warning systems be they magical or mundane. Chuck offered to take the first shift so that when he was done he could find himself a tree to climb. Even if it meant he woke up with a stiff back, that extra little bit of caution had already proven itself worth the effort, and his offer was met with unanimous agreement. The Bonecrushers had provisioned the friends with a week's worth of rations, so Stu didn't need to leave the protection of the fire to go hunt. Fresh meat was better than jerky, though, so he set out several snares in the hope of getting a rabbit or two for breakfast.

The fire crackled in the darkness as the friends huddled over mugs of tea. While the day had been bright and warm, once the sun went down a slight chill settled upon the air. TJ was first to break the post-supper silence. "I don't know about you guys, but I was starting to get used to having a roof over my head and a bed beneath my back."

The others nodded, with the exception of Stu, who replied. "Was getting kind of claustrophobic, to tell the truth. Being cooped up like that with all those other people." He shuddered. "I'm happy to be out on the road again."

Chuck looked incredulous at his claim and Allison snorted. "All those people? You live in an apartment complex, Stu. I've visited your sisters there. It may not be as big as the Bonecrushers' home, but it's got to be just as packed."

The other boys laughed but Stu looked thoughtful for a moment. He turned his gaze upward and continued as if Allison hadn't interrupted him, "And we don't need a roof overhead when there's no rain on the way. Not for a couple days, at least."

Jimmy raised his mug towards Stu in salute. "I agree. A dry night is a great night. Could be a lot colder too, don't you think, Allie? This time of year there's already snow on the ground in some places."

"Yeeeess," she replied slowly. "I'm sure that's true." Jimmy nodded, satisfied, and the group settled back into silence, eventually finding their way into bedrolls and off to sleep.

Morning came without incident, and Stu was pleased to find a pair of rabbits in his snares. He'd taken the last watch and had a stew burbling over the fire, ready to eat when the others woke. The friends packed up and began moving before the sun had crested the trees, traveling always further east. The shining sun and crisp air reminded them all of fall at home, and the only thing missing was the smell of grass being cut for the last time until spring. The lull of familiarity was almost enough for them to forget where they were and what they were doing. But the ominous presence of smoke on the trail ahead brought them all back to awareness of the dangers at hand in this new world they had found themselves in.

Stu, a dozen paces ahead, gestured to the right and the five immediately moved off the road to crouch in the nearby brush. Stu continued onward, his form becoming almost invisible in the undergrowth. After several long seconds the others followed along as quietly as possible, everyone suddenly glad for the boots Allison had received from the Goblins. She, herself, was positively amazed at the transformation. It seemed that her feet knew exactly where to land to avoid twigs, dead leaves, and anything else that might make noise. It was now her turn to wince at the noise when TJ or Jimmy placed a foot in the wrong place.

The source of the smoke was nearer than they had expected. After five minutes of walking Stu returned at a trot and motioned them forward urgently. Cresting a small rise they saw a hundred yards ahead of them a dozen or so covered wagons. Some were in the grass on either side of the road and the lead one was aflame. One of the burning wagon's axles appeared to be damaged as well, because although its horse was pulling for all it was worth in an attempt to escape the blaze, the vehicle wasn't budging. It was clear why no one was trying to put out the fire, or even trying to unhitch the poor horse from the burning wagon: twenty armed men, several on horseback, surrounded the caravan, weapons drawn as they shouted.

The friends looked at each other in uncertainty. Jimmy's eyes took on a strange look and his fists clenched and unclenched unconsciously. To Allison, he seemed itching for a fight, even if he didn't know who he was fighting, or why. She placed a hand on his shoulder and her touch calmed him down. He realized that that unless he was joined by his friends it wasn't a fight he could win. Stu nocked an arrow to his bow, just in case. "What do we do?" Allison whispered. Stu shrugged and TJ replied, "I don't know. Who are the good guys? If these are local soldiers apprehending criminals, we shouldn't get in the way."

"Assuming we like whoever's in charge here, that is," Chuck said wryly. The moments stretched out, no one willing to make a decision.

Remembering her ring, and knowing what effect it had on most people she met, Allison took matters into her own hands and stepped out from the woods. TJ grabbed at her arm but she slipped away smoothly and called out imperiously, "What's going on here? Who are you men and who are these people in the wagons?"

One of the horsemen turned his steed so that he could look at Allison. In contrast to the others who were dressed in breastplates or boiled leather, this man wore a full suit of chain-and-mail and was obviously in charge. He gestured toward one of the footmen, who ran over toward him. Just as the horseman bent over to speak, a man's voice rang out from inside one of the wagons, "Help! They're trying to rob us!" The leader glanced in the direction of the cry before turning back to the man at his side. After a brief exchange of words, the footman looked toward Allison, casually raised his bow, and sent an arrow flying directly toward her. Stunned at the sudden turn of events, she stood planted to the ground watching the arrow come. Just before it struck TJ collided with her and pulled her to the ground, the arrow passing harmlessly overhead.

"Well, I guess that solves that question, doesn't it? Bandits again." She smiled up at his face, inches from her own. "And thanks. I owe you one."

The situation having become clear, Stu wasted no time. His first arrow targeted the one who had fired at Allison, and it caught the bandit squarely in the chest. Surprised that his arrow pierced the man's breastplate, he made a mental note to thank Chuck again for discovering the magical bow in the kobold's compound. He scanned the battlefield, immediately noticing which of the bandits carried bows or crossbows and sending an arrow at each. Within moments there were five bowmen on the ground, three almost certainly dead and two incapacitated with arrows in an arm and a leg, respectively. One of the other bandits scrambled to reach a fallen comrade's bow, but the arrow Stu placed through his neck dissuaded any of the others from attempting the same sort of maneuver. The remaining attackers bolted for cover, placing the wagons between themselves and Stu's bow, but his job had been completed—his friends could close the distance between the woods and the wagons without being turned into pincushions.

Jimmy led the way forward, barely resisting the urge to charge ahead. With no archers left standing there wasn't any hurry. TJ and Allison marched behind him, with Chuck following at a bit of a distance. Meanwhile, Stu circled around the battlefield to flank their foes. As the others neared the first wagon, an arrow streaked just over Allison's shoulder into a bandit who had peeked out just a little too far from cover. She turned to glare at Stu, who, after giving her an exaggerated shrug, drew another arrow.

Circling around the wagons, the friends faced their remaining enemies. Even though Stu had taken out seven by himself, they were still outnumbered three to one. Four to one, thought Allison, if you didn't include her, since she wasn't much use in a fight. And even worse odds if you excluded Chuck as well. She glanced backward quickly and discovered he was no longer there. Excellent. The grins on their opponents' faces suggested that they had done the same math, and suddenly this didn't seem like such a good idea. It was, however, too late to turn back now, especially since Jimmy let out a battle roar and charged forward, his enormous sword raised over his head.

The nearest enemy stepped to meet him, his own (smaller) sword held at the ready. On his left arm hung a round shield of wood banded in iron, which he raised to ward off Jimmy's first blow. The shield was no match for the fury of Jimmy's initial assault, however, and instead of clang of steel there was a groaning tear as the metal-reinforced wood split down the middle. The man let out a cry and fell to the ground, arm crushed and useless, his body going into shock.

A yell from the side drew Jimmy's attention to a horse bearing down upon him. The rider's long spear was aimed directly for his chest. Before the beast was able to close the entire distance, balls of magical force raced out from TJ's outstretched hand. The projectiles all collided with the rider, throwing him out of the saddle and onto the ground with a loud crack. The bandit lay there, unmoving, smoke rising from his chest. The horse, rather than completing the charge, slowed, stopped, and after looking around in momentary confusion, began cropping the grass.

In just those few moments, the bandits' confident grins had been shifted into something different. On some faces was uncertainty, on others, wariness. Realizing that this would be more of a fight than they expected, the bandits spread out slightly. Four approached Jimmy at once, still mindful of Stu's arrows and keeping close to wagons for cover. Visions of the kobold attack, during which their large friend was beaten not through skill but by sheer numbers, came to Allison unbidden. TJ seemed to have similar thoughts and began to chant a complex series of syllables. Blue light shot forth from his hands and into Jimmy. The mystic glow encompassed the larger man's body, and while TJ looked shaken from the exertion, its effects on Jimmy were astounding. His movements, elegant and fluid before, became almost otherworldly. He was no longer merely quick. He was *fast.*

The magic caused momentary confusion in the ranks of the attackers, and Jimmy used it to his advantage. Twirling left, his sword arced out at his first opponent, smacking the man's shield aside and leaving him unprotected for a follow up slash along his torso. The breastplate offered no protection from the enchanted sword in Jimmy's hand. One down. Continuing his spin, he drove a shoulder into the next in line. Adrenaline and mass won out over the leather jerkin the man was wearing, and his ribs crunched in the impact. A follow-up elbow to the face crushed his nose and dropped him into unconsciousness. Two down. He spun, his sword slicing through the neck of the third man and then skewering the fourth, all before any of them could process his movements. Jimmy himself seemed surprised at how quickly he was moving as he danced into the second rank of foes.

One of the bandits had managed to recover a massive crossbow from a fallen comrade and he fired it at Jimmy from a mere twenty feet away. The magical chain armor could only do so much, and the loud TWANG was followed by an equally loud THUNK. Jimmy spun in his tracks, the bolt planted firmly in his left shoulder, just above his heart. The large man fell to his knees, grimacing in pain. Allison let out a cry of alarm, knowing that if he had been struck just an inch or two lower her friend would be dead. The bowman frantically worked at the crank to reset his weapon for a second, killing blow. TJ, exhaustion from his last expenditure of power clear on his face, extended a hand and directed a ball of fire towards the man. The explosion sent both the crossbowman and two of his comrades flying like rag dolls.

"Get to Jimmy," he grunted, raised his arms in front of him, and mouthed more arcane words. A wall of flames sprung up between where their friend lay bleeding and the remaining enemies before TJ collapsed, his eyes rolling back into his head. Allison used the cover from the flames to rush over to Jimmy so that she could heal his wound. As she ran, another of Stu's arrows flew past her, a grunt indicating that he had once again found his mark.

"You're on your own, Ben," a voice called out from beyond the wall of flame, followed by the sound of voices in muttered agreement and footsteps retreating in haste.

"Get back here, you cowards! Come back!" The frustration in the voice made clear that they were not listening to his request.

Allison looked at Jimmy's wound, grateful that he had been shot at such close range. The crossbow was so powerful that the bolt's tip had not just pierced his armor, but gone through his shoulder and out the other side. The point had a wicked barb on it, and if she had been forced to pull it out, it would have caused massive bleeding.

Allison snapped off the fletching and said, "Hold still a moment." Grasping the arrow where it emerged from his back, she gave a yank, sliding it through his shoulder the rest of the way. Jimmy grunted in pain and jerked, causing Allison to lose her grip on the shaft. The arrow's point sliced her fingers open and blood welled up in her hand. Pain shot up her arm all the way to her shoulder, but it took only a moment's concentration to send healing through her arm to close the wound and dull the pain.

The holes in both front and back of Jimmy's shoulder began to bleed in earnest as well, now that the bolt had been removed. The last time she'd needed to fix a life-threatening wound was when TJ had been stabbed, not long after they had crossed from their world into this one, and it had been an act of desperation. This time she paid more attention to the process and, as the energy flowed up from the earth, through her, and into Jimmy's shoulder, she could feel the blood vessels closing, the muscles and tendons repairing themselves, and ultimately the holes in his skin sealing themselves. It felt to her almost like dissecting a frog in biology class, but in reverse. It felt amazing, and she suddenly understood the exhilaration TJ felt after using his own arcane power. A wave of exhaustion rolled through her. She hoped with practice the fatigue would be less of an issue. She also hoped she wouldn't need to practice very much.

Jimmy's eyes opened and he gave Allison a nod of thanks. His eyes suddenly opened wider in surprise, their gaze focused behind her. She turned to look and discovered the bandit leader towering over her, his sword poised to strike. He smiled a cruel smile at her and said, "Good. I wanted you to see me before you die. It will be my consolation for all of this."

His arm began its descent but she had no energy to dodge the coming blow. The blue light surrounding Jimmy had faded, and with his own wound he would never be able to get up in time to parry. TJ was drained and if Stu hadn't shot this guy yet, he must be distracted by other things or did not have a line of sight. She closed her eyes and waited for the blow to fall, only to snap them back open at the sound of Chuck's voice.

"Surprise!"

The bandit's eyes turned glassy and he slumped forward, his sword clattering to the ground next to Allison. Chuck's dagger was planted firmly between the man's shoulder blades.

"Phew. Good timing, Chuckles." Jimmy staggered to his feet and rotated his injured shoulder as he surveyed the scene, pleased that all their enemies were killed or had fled. With his other arm he extended a hand to the still-shaken Allison and helped her to her feet.

"Thanks," Chuck replied with a little bow. "Been workin' on it." Pointing into the distance he added, "What about the ones that got away? We going to go after them?" By this time Stu had approached, and at Chuck's suggestion he turned to scan the woods for signs of the men who ran.

TJ spoke up, "Nah, let them go. They won't be back for more, and maybe the word will spread that this part of the world isn't safe for their type. At least while we're here, that is."

The others nodded and got to work cleaning weapons

and armor, retrieving arrows, and in Chuck's case, rifling the bodies for anything of value. As they worked, Stu asked TJ, "That wall of fire was pretty cool, and that was some great timing. But what was that thing you did to Jimmy? I've never even heard of that sort of spell. Where'd that come from?"

"It was a haste spell. I don't know the exact calculations, but I think it increased his speed by just about double. Twice the attacks, twice the movement, twice the reflexes. We couldn't have faked that or the wall spells back in the real world, at least not easily, so they were never incorporated into the game." With a wry smile he continued, "Obviously things are different here. I learned them over the last week from Egg. He wasn't joking when he said he'd been studying for decades. It's amazing how much lore he's been able to squeeze into that tiny head. He also had an extensive library with quite a few ancient spell books. These were ones that he suggested I look at while we were visiting. I need to be careful though. They take a lot out of me, and I probably shouldn't be casting both at the same time like that if I can help it. I suspect with experience it will become easier. The energy balls I cast barely tire me at all."

Allison sighed. "I wish I had thought to do some practicing, too."

TJ shook his head. "Healing magic doesn't work like that, I'm afraid. No spell books and practicing."

"Then how do I get more spells? Healing and smite are boring."

"Not to us they aren't," countered Jimmy with a grin and tapped his injured shoulder. Allison was only a little surprised to see that her friend's armor had magically healed itself as well.

TJ nodded enthusiastically before explaining, "When Healers gain a level in the game up they just get a couple new magic abilities. I don't know how that translates here though. With all we've done since we got here, you should definitely have levelled up." He shook his head. "I guess we'll see what you can do when you try to do it."

Engrossed in what they were doing, they all actually jumped a little bit when a shaky voice issued from one of the wagons. "Milady? Is it safe to go and put out that fire yet?"

Allison beamed a smile at the face peeking out from a wagon's canvas flap. "Yeah, why don't you do that now."

CHAPTER 3

Once the all clear was sounded, a flurry of activity took place around the wagons, beginning with extinguishing the fire. There was no water nearby, so the waggoneers beat at the blaze with blankets, smothering it through brute force. Some of those not actively fighting the fire helped unhitch the poor horse, which was neighing and rolling its eyes in fear, both from the smoke and the smell of blood that permeated the area. Others gave the bodies that Chuck had searched a second pass, relieving them of armor, weapons, and other items that Chuck had judged too bulky or of too little value to bother with. The burned wagon itself had taken too much damage to be salvaged, but much of its cargo was in good enough shape to be unloaded and placed into other wagons. The final chore was the gruesome task of dragging the attackers' bodies off the road and into the nearby trees to be left in a pile for wolves. In light of the morning's chaos and the understandable anxiety of the horses, the decision had also been made to not travel further that day. Even so, no one wanted to camp at the battle site, so the business of establishing a camp waited until they had moved along the road a few hundred yards.

All of the work was directed by a man who looked to be in his mid-fifties, and only after the camp was established in its new spot did he approach the five friends. They sat huddled together out of the way of the activity, still a little worn out from the battle. TJ made to stand up to greet him, but the man waved him back down and said, "No, no, don't get up. You've done plenty already. I'm not the type to take offense at someone sitting in my presence." He chuckled. "And I'm certainly not as exalted as your ladyship." He added, then gave Allison a slight bow. She couldn't quite decide if it was meant to be ironic.

"Anyway, my name is Thaddeus. I'm caravan master for this group. You have our thanks," he said with another bow. "Those fellas had us pretty well done for. About when you got here we were just hoping to get out of it with our lives."

Chuck spoke up. "Hey, no sweat. That's what we do, I guess. We're like the Avengers or something." Thaddeus gave a quizzical look, and Chuck pressed on without explanation. "What were you doing out here without protection anyway? That doesn't really seem particularly safe, if you ask me. Heck, if I had seen you out here all alone I would have thought about robbing you, myself!" Despite the little man's grin, the caravan master's face said that he didn't appreciate the joke. Allison gave his shoulder a slap. "In another life, that is," Chuck finished weakly.

"Ahem. Well. We normally would have had guards with us, but times are hard and sell swords are more expensive than they used to be. The ones we could have picked up at the last town looked just as likely to rob us themselves as to guard us, so we thought that maybe if we were quick we could sneak on through this leg to Providence City. There, we might be able to join up with a larger group and hire some more…trustworthy…protection." He nodded to where the bodies were piled up. "Turns out we were right about the first part at least. Most of our attackers were the 'guards' we'd considered hiring." He sighed. "You know, I knew that the one called Ben was trouble the moment I set eyes on him. The way he treated the others around him wasn't how a true captain would act. I think this crew was all with him out of desperation." He paused, a thoughtful look on his face. "Anyway, we're bunking down here for the day, and the least we can offer you is a nice hot meal and some company before you continue on to wherever you're headed. Where *are* you folks headed?"

The five exchanged glances, unsure of how much to tell him about their plans. Finally, Allison broke the silence and said, "We're headed east. We don't have a specific destination in mind and are just sort of seeing what comes our way." Everything she said was technically correct, so she didn't feel like she was really lying. Whether or not her magical ring made her more convincing, the older man nodded his head as if what she said made perfect sense. Maybe there were small bands of adventurers all over this world, picking a direction and then just walking in search of something to fight. Only then remembering what he had said about sell swords, it occurred to her that the next time she had to explain what they were up to, the role of "mercenary band" would probably be a better cover than "We're just headed east."

"Well then how about you come along with us?" He offered, taking a knee so that he wouldn't be standing over them. "We're headed east too, and Providence City is as good a destination as any, particularly if you don't have anywhere in mind. Given how easily you rescued us, we probably can't pay you what you're worth, but the city is only another couple days away, and I bet it won't be much work." He chuckled. "Even if there are more bandits hiding in these woods, word of what you have done is going to be spread by those men you let escape. This is going to be the easiest, most peaceful caravan trip we've ever had."

Again, the friends looked at each other, but this time it was TJ who spoke up. "Yes, I think we'd like that. Having some company would be nice, and I welcome the chance to get a full night's sleep while someone else watches."

Chuck chimed in, "Now about that pay…"

"Oh come ON, Chuck. Really?" Allison gave him an irritated look before she noticed the sly grin on his face. Thaddeus looked bemusedly back and forth at the exchange, until Allison followed up with, "We don't need your money. Your company and your food is plenty." They all knew that the wealth they'd been given by the Bonecrushers was worth a small ransom in gold and in comparison, the traders had nothing of value to offer them. Besides, they all hoped to be home long before they had the chance to spend all their money.

The old man looked perplexed, and asked, "Are you sure? We really don't mind paying you. If it weren't for you, we'd have nothing left at all. And guard fees are in the budget, anyway."

"Nope, we're good. But we thank you for the offer!" Allison did her best to come across as magnanimous, hoping the ring would help.

"OK, if you say so." Thaddeus didn't look convinced. "Well let's see if we can't get something good cooked up for dinner tonight. We still have some venison, and we've got plenty of beans and some potatoes. We'll cook up a stew and break out a cask of ale and have ourselves a good meeting with new friends!" He raised his voice for that last bit and a cheer erupted from the other caravan workers, who had been expecting another night of travel rations. Turning to face the camp, he directed, "Wilhelm, Edgar, go and fetch some firewood. Cookie, get what you need and get a choppin'."

Two men trotted off into the woods at his words. An older man missing several teeth said, "OK, boss!" and began to rummage through one of the wagons.

Jimmy murmured, "His name is Cookie? Really?" He shook his head. "And look at him, almost straight out of an old western. I didn't realize people like that actually existed."

TJ, in a distracted, scholarly voice, said, "Well, technically, they don't. If this is a fictional world, then I guess we would expect certain archetypes to manifest themselves in way that seems unrealistic to us. And that is, after all, the point. This isn't meant to be realistic."

Surprised, Jimmy turned to his friend and replied, "Whoa, TJ, did you hear what you just said? We need to get out of here, and fast. You're turning into a total egghead, and I don't think I like it."

TJ blushed and muttered something, then stood up and walked a short way from the campsite.

"We're all changing," Allison said. "We really need to get out of here."

Thaddeus looked back and forth between them, trying to keep up with the conversation. When silence fell he said, "Well I have no idea what you're talking about." He stood up, and then went to see what Cookie was doing, giving a couple of worried looking backward glances.

Chuck let out a small giggle. "Well that's one way to make an impression! I'm betting that when it's our turn to keep watch, he's not going to be sleeping so easily. We really ought to remember that to everyone but us five, this is a completely normal life." The others nodded their heads then fell into silence, each lost in their own thoughts.

When the stew was cooked, everyone hunkered down by the fire on stools pulled from the back of a wagon. Instead of bowls they used small, hollowed out loaves of sourdough bread for the stew, so even after all of the meat and vegetables were gone there was still plenty for each person to eat. After a time, the cask of ale was brought out and mugs handed around.

Allison took her mug but looked at it uncertainly. "Um, aren't we too young for this?" She asked her friends. "I don't even have my license yet." Jimmy shrugged and let his character take over, filling and draining the mug twice before letting out a massive belch and an, "Ahhh, that hit the spot. Not like what my gramps would brew back home, but still pretty good."

"Your gramps?" Stu raised an eyebrow.

"Yeah, up in the hills. Don't have barley and oats and stuff up there, so we use whatever we can find. It's got quite a tang to it, it does."

Thaddeus, happy with some more normal conversation, said, "Well cheers to that and cheers to your gramps," then drank down his own mug, a satisfied smile on his face.

Eager to change the conversation from drinking to anything else, Allison turned to the caravan master and asked, "So, tell us about this Providence City. What's it like?"

He looked shocked. "What's it like? Really? You've never heard of Providence City?"

She looked over to the boys, wondering if maybe they were supposed to know about it from game lore. They returned only shrugs in response. It was funny that TJ could remember the smallest piece of information about the ring she had found but didn't know things about the world's major cities. Funny, but inconvenient. They needed to blend in, and things like not knowing major cities and their discussions about the "real world," weren't helping.

Noticing the looks of surprise all around the campfire, Chuck blurted out, "Well of course we've heard of Providence City. I mean, who hasn't? But none of us have spent much time out of our own homes to the west. And it sounds like you've done all sorts of traveling. So what's it *like*? What will we see when we get there? What will we experience?"

Chuck's quick thinking covered for their ignorance,

and Thaddeus nodded before beginning to speak in earnest. "What is it like?" He repeated. "What isn't it like is a better question! There are a hundred thousand souls living inside the walls, and another twenty in the surrounding countryside. There are tanners and smiths and jewelers and more food vendors and taverns than you can imagine. Even got lots of people like your friend with the bow, so he'll fit right in." The older man noticed a change in the friends' mood at the reference to Stu's skin color, so he pressed ahead quickly. "They have a standing militia of about five thousand, not including the city watch, and could raise five more in conscripts in relatively short order. They've got political relationships with a number of other cities of similar size but their military is the biggest around, so they are generally looked to as the one to follow when big decisions need to be made.

"Now just recently this new group of folks have moved in." He nodded towards Jimmy and continued, "Some of your folks, maybe. They came down from the north and pitched their tents right outside the walls. It's like a miniature city right outside the city—there's got to be close to ten thousand living there—men, women, and children. They brought their markets, their artisans, their *everything*. And if that weren't enough to cause chaos within the city, every single one of those men, women, and children knows how to fight. They give their children their first swords when they turn five and start training boys and girls both in earnest by the age of seven." At this, Jimmy smiled wistfully at childhood memories the description elicited. "So, you can imagine that things were a little tense at first, when a small army showed up at the gates and decided to set up camp. Luckily, cool heads prevailed on both sides and they have settled into what could be called an understanding. The tent folks keep to themselves and don't cause a ruckus in town and the town folks won't try to drive them off. Truth is, if it came down to a fight, no one would win. There'd be a lot of dead bodies on either side, and even if the Providencers managed to finish the tenters off, the city would be left undefended. It wouldn't take long for some other force to march in and capture the city." Thaddeus took another drink from his cup, then continued in a softer voice, "In fact, with what's been going on with the Arcanum and all, the city leaders are scared to death."

"The Arcanum?" TJ asked. "Why do they care about what's going on in the East?"

Thaddeus smiled grimly. "The only ones who don't care what's going on in the east are fools and dead men. You don't strike me as the former, and I imagine you'd rather not join the ranks of the latter. The Arcanum is nearly unified behind this power-hungry wizard and now he can start looking west. Unless I miss my guess, he will be ready to move in force within a year." Some of the others around the campfire nodded their heads in agreement.

"Would it really be that bad?" TJ followed up. "My own masters at the Collegium were reasonable enough, at least when they weren't rapping my knuckles with sticks. Not to mention wise. I could think of fates a lot worse than being governed by wizards."

The old man shook his head in disbelief. "If that's truly what you got from your schooling, your masters are far less wise than you give them credit for. Imagine a wizard with the battle lust of a barbarian and the ruthlessness of the blackest assassin. Only such a one could force the others of his kind into submission." His eyes bored into TJ's from across the fire, his brow furrowed. "I can't think of much worse than being ruled by one like him." TJ gulped and nodded his agreement.

"So, what are the Providencers planning on doing?" Jimmy said, breaking the uncomfortable silence. "Are they getting ready to fight?"

Thaddeus spat into the fire. "Some of them are actually considering throwing their lot in with this Magnus." Seeing Allison's horrified look, he added, "They want to be on the winning side, you know. They could stand up to him, and maybe win, but again, their defenses would be devastated and they would be easy pickings for another city-state further west. Or, with the size of their army, they could tip the balance in his favor. Between his magic and their swords, few could stand against them."

This last admission caused the friends to look at each other anxiously. They knew he had enlisted Crackrock the ogre to be his tool, so an alliance with Providence City could already be in the works. Their visible anxiety at the thought wasn't lost on Thaddeus or his men. The old man quickly continued, "The way I look at it, I just want my people to be safe. We aren't taking sides, ourselves. And you know, it's been a couple months since we last passed through, so I'm curious to find out what news there is. One thing's for sure, there's always something interesting going on in place like Providence." There was a murmur of agreement from the others around the fire.

Chuck looked around slyly and said, "Sounds like my kind of city."

Thaddeus gave him an appraising glance and said, "Yes, something makes me think that it is."

"Sweet."

CHAPTER 4

The friends settled into the caravan's routine over the next several days. Stu had commandeered one of the bandits' horses and rode it easily, though the others preferred to ride on or walk alongside the wagons. They travelled fully armed and armored, and slept with weapons handy even when not on sentry duty. Though the likelihood of getting ambushed again was remote, none of them were willing to take the risk of being caught unawares. Each evening Stu set his snares and spent the hour right after sunset hunting for deer. Their second night on the road he returned with one, much to the delight of the rest of the travelers.

Days passed uneventfully until they approached the area claimed by Providence City, when Thaddeus called Stu back from his hunt.

"Technically, we're in unclaimed territory. But that's only technically, and if one of the wardens decided to come roving out this far and accused you of poaching, I don't think that 'technically' would have a lot of sway in front of the magistrate, if you get what I mean. We've only got another day or two on the road, and we can survive on basic rations."

Stu grunted his reply, "Meh. If the forest is wild, then it's wild. Not like any warden could track me anyway." Even so, after setting his snares he returned to the camp.

"They gonna need papers, Tad?" It was Wilhelm who spoke up as they sat around the fire that evening.

"Papers. Hrm. I hadn't thought of that." The caravan master stroked his chin a moment. "I'm guessing that you're not the type to have travel papers issued by one of the local governments?" He paused only a moment before continuing with a sigh, "Of course you aren't. I really should have thought of that before now. Well here's the thing." He looked around the circle at each of the friends in turn. "Anyone can get through the main gate. There's no way they could regulate the comings and goings of that many people. There are some parts of the city, however, where only locals, or those who have other governments vouch for them, are allowed."

"What sorts of areas?" Allison asked.

"Some of the more specialized merchants. Government offices. The places where those of means congregate." He rubbed a thumb against two of his fingers.

"Shame we didn't know about that before now," TJ said. "Not that we really planned to visit anywhere like that, but it would have been nice to have the option."

"What do these papers look like?" Chuck leaned forward, his eyes alight. "I suspect you have some for yourselves?"

Thaddeus smiled. "Of course we do, and you're

welcome to take a look at them if you'd like. Wilhelm, it was your idea, so how about you go and get them from the chest? Including some of the special ones." He gave the other man a wink.

"You bet, boss." Everyone around the fire waited patiently while the man went to Thaddeus's wagon to dig around. He returned with a stack of papers and handed Chuck most of them. They looked like typical government documents, with seals and signatures and lots of writing in complex words. The first was Thaddeus's, followed by Wilhelm's and the rest of the caravan drivers'.

Chuck flipped through the stack, his experienced eyes noting where the colors and textures of the paper differed, as well as subtle variations in the quality of the seals. Thaddeus looked on in amusement as Chuck smelled and even tasted a few, finally looking up and asking, "So which of these is a real one? The calligraphy is the same on all, so whoever forged them has a talented hand."

"Mine is a real one, of course. Caravan masters are the types of people towns want to come visiting, so I had no trouble getting mine. There are a couple others there that are authentic, but I had about half of them professionally," he gave a discrete cough, "made. Wilhelm, would you hand him the remaining ones?"

Chuck took the offered documents, and was pleased to note that none of them had names filled in. "Well isn't that convenient?" He quipped.

"I have found that it is, yes," Thaddeus confirmed. "You never know what…or who will need to be transported from point A to point B, so I have always found it to be useful to prepare for…how should I put it? Nontraditional circumstances. Since you refused to take our coin in payment for your services, perhaps we could arrange a barter transaction instead? I would be more than happy to arrange for you to all have your own papers before we get to Providence City. Cookie is not just a fine chef, but he has a way with ink, as well."

The turn of this conversation made Allison anxious. "Um, guys? Is that really the sort of thing that we want to get involved with? Aren't we supposed to be on the good guy's side? And what if we get caught? What would happen to us? Do we want an entire city to know our faces and be out to get us?"

Chuck smirked at her concern, having in fact had an entire city out to get him at least once before in his past career. Stu waved his arm in irritation, still upset about not being able to go out hunting. Of the five, he was the one most obviously influenced by his "character," perhaps because they had been spending so much time in the wilderness, where he felt most at home. More than once Allison got the impression that he only returned from his evening hunting trips out of obligation and not any actual desire to make the trip to Providence City.

TJ and Jimmy exchanged a look, communicating silently with each other. Despite being polar opposites in terms of character archetype and temperament, they both had the "complete the mission" attitude common among role playing gamers. While not quite as mercenary as Chuck, they recognized the importance of taking advantage of opportunities when they arose. If the story gives you a way to bypass a problem, do it.

At last TJ spoke. "I think we should take the papers,

assuming Chuck considers the work to be good enough that we won't get into any trouble. None of us should have any illusions regarding his past career, and if he thinks the documents of sufficient quality, I am willing to accept his judgment. I have been thinking deeply over these last several days about what we should be doing and where we should be. It is clear to me that our mission," he paused a moment to be sure that everyone knew he was being intentionally vague and the details were none of the caravan workers' business before continuing, "requires us to have a more specific plan than simply 'go east.' I have developed some ideas as to what sorts of specifics we could pursue, and having access to the elite of this town could very well be of value." Noticing the look of frustration on Allison's face, he added, "I understand your point of view, and in general I don't condone this sort of behavior. That said, in the grand scheme of relative mischief, this ranks pretty low and it's entirely possible that a great good might come of it."

She looked at Jimmy. "Well?"

"Yeah, pretty much what he said, but with smaller words." He belched, then took another swig from his mug.

"Well do we have to forge them?" Allison continued to press the point. "Why can't we just apply to get papers the regular way? How did you get yours, Thaddeus?"

"Oh, I applied when I first started driving the wagons. I guess that was back in eighty-six or so?" One of the wagon drivers nodded in agreement. "I wasn't native and didn't have a sponsor, so the town guard asked around all over the place, people I knew, people I'd done business with, that sort of thing. Amazingly thorough investigation, to be sure. They somehow managed to find people that had been avoiding me for years. Folks who owed me money, you know. Anyway, after I had filed my request I took the caravan out and down the coast a bit. When I got back three months later, it was just about done. I only had to wait about for a week more or so before they made it official." He snorted. "Still didn't collect my money from those folks they found, though."

"It took you *three months* to get your paperwork?" Allison asked, disbelief plastered across her face.

The old man nodded. "Yup, and I was one of the lucky ones. I'd done business off and on in Providence City for years before running the caravans on my own, so they didn't have to look too hard to find people to put in a good word about me."

"How many references do you need? Or sponsors? Would you be able to do that for us?"

Thaddeus looked uncomfortable at her request. "The truth of the matter is that my one word isn't going to do a whole lot of good. I'm just a guest, not a citizen, so I don't even think they would let me sponsor anyone. That so, Oswald?" The man who had nodded earlier grunted agreement. "And we're awful grateful for what you've done for us, but in truth we've only just met you. I'd be happy to tell them how you saved our lives and ran off those bandits, but don't think it would make a whole lot of difference."

TJ chimed in, "And we don't have three months to wait." He looked over to where Stu sat glowering, staring off into the woods. "I don't even want to imagine what things will be like in three months. We've got to get this done soon, if it's going to get done at all."

Allison looked exasperated. "OK. I don't see how this could possibly end well, but I guess I've been overruled." She glared at TJ. "Remember, this whole thing was your idea. If I end up rotting in a dungeon somewhere—with or without a dragon in it—I'm going to be really angry at you, 'k?"

"Hey, we've got Chuckles. What could possibly go wrong?"

"Then it's settled," Chuck said. His voice took on a businesslike tone. "Now, no offense to Cookie, but I could do better work than this without my hands." The caravan's forger looked mildly offended but shrugged it off. "Thaddeus, you say yours is the real deal? Cause that's pretty important."

"Yes, mine is absolutely authentic." Chuck studied his face for a few moments before nodding.

"Ok, then I've got to get to work. I assume you've got brushes and inks and the like, right?"

"Right over here." Cookie led him back to the wagon. He lit a lamp and hung it on a peg before pulling out a drawer from one of the benches. With a wink at Chuck, he removed a false bottom revealing the supplies. "So, if you're really as good as you say, would you mind if I watched you work?" After a pause, he challenged, "Been a long time since I met anyone even half as good as me."

Chuck shrugged his agreement. "Sure thing. If we've only got a day or so, let's get moving on it now. No way I'm doing this in the back of a wagon rolling over cobbles, so we've got a couple late nights ahead of us." He removed all of the materials, inspecting each. Most were to his satisfaction, but a couple of the brushes and one pot of ink he tossed aside, saying, "Junk. Junk. Junk." At Cookie's look he added, "Those brushes have the wrong hair for this sort of work, and that ink will fade the first time the papers get wet. Not the sort of thing you want in an official document meant to last a long time." He climbed up into the wagon, spread some blank parchments in front of him on the bench, placed Thaddeus's original right in the middle, and got to work.

The others returned to chatting around the campfire, but Allison's heart wasn't in it. After just a few minutes of half-listening she excused herself to go bed down for the night, claiming it had been a long day. The sounds from around the campfire diminished to nothing as she slipped into unconsciousness, but one voice followed her into her dreams, loud and clear. It was TJ's. "What could possibly go wrong?"

CHAPTER 5

Dust from the gathered throng that made up the line the caravan was stuck in clogged their lungs and set the friends to spasms of choking. The midday sun beat down on them from overhead and beads of sweat lined their brows. They had approached the gates two hours before, but because of some problem up ahead, they had been required to just sit and wait. Allison, having regained her spirits since the forgery discussion, was sitting on the back of one of the wagons, enjoying its shade as her feet dangled freely over the side and munching on a piece of leftover roasted rabbit. Stu's snares had been particularly effective the night before and with the pancakes and bacon they had cooked up there was enough for lunch and maybe even an afternoon snack. With Providence City on the horizon and with it the promise of replenished stores, Thaddeus had allowed them to splurge on a big breakfast.

"It's not always like this." The caravan master had approached from the front of the line and startled her when he spoke. "Most days, it's much easier. The guards have two lines: one for caravans like ours and one for smaller groups and individuals. They discovered that the larger merchants tended to have fewer issues, so for us it ought to be a very brief process. They'll ask us what we're carrying, assess an import duty if need be, and let us go on in. People like us have too much to lose by doing something and getting caught, so they don't have to watch us too closely."

Allison asked, "But doesn't that end up becoming self-defeating? If the large caravans don't get checked as closely as the smaller merchants, doesn't that make the large caravans more likely to do something wrong? Like forging papers for getting into places they don't belong?"

"Well I never said the system was perfect." He winked at her. "You know, so long as they're willing to let us do our stuff and harass someone else, I'm not going to complain if their logic doesn't make sense."

Allison giggled. "Fair enough, I guess."

"So…where are you folks from?" Thaddeus looked sideways at her, trying to sound nonchalant, but it didn't work.

"West." Her terse reply ended the conversation, and the older man took the hint. He shrugged and wandered back toward the front of the group.

Not long after, the wagons began to move again, and as they approached their turn in line, Chuck handed each of his companions their own copy of the travel papers. To their eyes, they looked like nothing special, but Cookie was looking at Chuck with reverence. "I tell ya, boss," he murmured to Thaddeus. "I've never seen anything like it, how good those are, and how fast he did 'em. That kid's got some talent."

Chuck gave a mock bow and a wink and then instructed everyone. "The papers were issued a year or so ago—I had to use the same signature as Thaddeus's and it would be a problem if that guy had died before the dates on the ones we're using. I've already given them some creases and aged them, but it wouldn't hurt to work 'em over in your hands a bit as well. If anyone asks, you got 'em in bulk as part of a caravan's escort, and you don't remember any of the details. Everyone got it?" The other four nodded their understanding and then went to work personalizing the creases in their papers as they walked.

Finally, it was their turn at the gate, and Allison saw first-hand what Thaddeus had told her about the two lines. It seemed that the people in the other line had barely moved at all while their caravan crossed the last half mile or so to the gates. The gates themselves, along with the rest of the city's walls, were made from tightly mortared, small dull brown stones each perhaps a foot square. At intervals along the crenelated wall were places that looked to have been patched with newer stones, as if the spots had been damaged during a siege. It was hard to tell from their vantage point how thick the wall itself was, though it was wide enough for sentries to walk along the top. The gate house was flanked by towers, each of which extended above the height of the wall by a dozen feet or so and offered arrow slits from which defenders could shoot. Altogether, it looked like whoever had designed the city's outer defenses knew what they were doing.

The guards at the entrance looked bored and disinterested in their jobs, waving some people through without a second glance and then seemingly at random picking out others for thorough searches. Thaddeus went up to the officer in charge and handed him the travel papers for his caravans' workers, then leaned in closely to speak more quietly. The bundle that changed hands seemed a little bulkier than it should have, and Allison noticed the officer placing something from the stack into his pocket, looking over towards the guardhouse as he did. Maybe it was the caravan's ability to pay bigger bribes that moved this line along, she thought, rather than there being fewer "issues," as Thaddeus had put it.

Thaddeus turned back toward the wagons and pointed in the friends' direction, then waved them forward. Once they approached, he introduced them to the gate guard. "This is Lieutenant Caldwell. He'll take a look at your papers and make sure they're all in order."

The friends each handed the officer their papers and he looked through them casually, seemingly content that everything was in order. Allison suspected that they could have given him notes from their mothers and he would have still passed them through. The golden rule—he who has the gold makes the rules—was hard at work here.

As the officer began to hand back their papers a voice spoke up from the side. "Lieutenant. Will you please empty your pockets?" Caldwell's face got a hunted look on it and his neck snapped around as he looked for a way to escape. Two sets of hands grabbed his arms from either side, however, holding him firmly in place.

Thaddeus, looking completely unconcerned, turned to the newcomer and gave a slight bow. "Ahh, Captain. I'm sure this is just an unfortunate coincidence that has landed us here right as you were taking this fellow into custody. He had just inspected our papers and those of our guards, and was about to pass us through. May we continue?"

The guard captain looked at him stone-faced and said, "Papers, please?"

"Well as I said, this fellow had already inspected them, though I'm happy to oblige." He handed the papers over with a confident face, and the captain looked through them. He squinted at a number of them, and then took the ones that Caldwell still held in his hand. He flipped back and forth between them, nodding his head here and there, and then said, "If you will excuse me for a moment, I must check something with my superiors, and really shouldn't leave the lieutenant standing out here any longer." He gave a quick salute, gestured to the two men securing Caldwell, and disappeared back into the guard tower with the papers.

"Well, this is not what I expected," Thaddeus said, scratching his chin and trying not to look worried. "Though it's not like we have really done anything wrong. All I was doing was greasing the wheels a little bit, and that in and of itself isn't illegal."

They waited about five minutes, shifting their weight back and forth from foot to foot until the captain came back out of the tower, the two soldiers that had taken Caldwell into custody flanking him. He approached them, his face still solemn and their travel papers in his hand. "So, these are your papers, yes?"

"If those are the ones you took from the lieutenant, they are." Thaddeus continued to project confidence.

"Well then you must all come with me. These are all forgeries, and we don't take kindly to folks like you trying to bribe your way in. Maybe that worked in the past, but not anymore." The long delay in what was normally a fast-moving line suddenly made sense. Allison wondered how many other groups like theirs had been detained, in just the same way.

One of the soldiers stepped forward to take Thaddeus's arms, and another reached out to grab Allison. Jimmy reached over his shoulder to draw his sword, but Chuck's hand snatched at his arm and pulled it back. The smaller man gave his head a shake and flicked his glance to the wall above the guardhouse. A dozen bowmen stood with arrows drawn, an officer standing ready to give the command to fire. Jimmy grimaced and let his hand fall limp.

As they allowed themselves to be disarmed and led into the guardhouse, Allison's eyes shot daggers at TJ. "What could possibly go wrong, huh?"

Interlude

"My Lord, I have news from the west." The kneeling steward looked up expectantly at the wizard-king upon his elevated throne, He had done well in the man's service, but experience had told him it was no more than luck. Others in the wizard's employ had been banished, tortured or executed almost at random, even when they had been successful at their assigned tasks. He had long since resigned himself to this life, however.

Rumors told of how, early in his reign, some of those

who displeased the wizard tried to flee his service. No matter how well they had hidden themselves, in short order they had been returned to his presence to face punishment. And the less said about that, the better. No, serving this madman was his lot in life, however long that life might be. As such, his voice was strong and confident. He would either die this day or he would not. His fate was completely out of his hands.

The wizard Magnus looked down at his servant with a smile, absently rubbing the gold-and-jeweled armrest of his throne. His robes today were of the finest silk and lace, as befitted one of his stature. Layers of purples blended with reds and blues, and embroidery of gold and silver thread was accented by diamonds and rubies. If it were possible for something to outshine the glory of Magnus' throne, his robes were the things to do it. The blankness in his eyes belied the smile on his face. This was a man whose emotions were completely unreadable.

"You may speak," he granted magnanimously with a wave of his arm.

The servant swallowed unconsciously. "I regret to inform you, oh Great One, that one of your champions has been defeated."

The wizard raised a single eyebrow. "Oh really?" he asked. Leaning forward and resting his elbows on his knees he continued, "Please tell me more."

"Well, my Exalted Lord, the ogre, Crackrock, has been slain. His kobold minions have fled their redoubt, and most were killed by local militias over subsequent weeks. We've lost our foothold in the mountain."

Magnus leaned back in his seat and stroked his neatly groomed beard. "Is that so?"

"Yes, Great One." The servant bobbed his head several times, and in a fit of worry dropped to his knees. Resigned to his fate as he was, he was more than willing to debase himself in front of this lunatic if it meant another day of life. There would be a feast tonight in the senior servant's quarters, with wine, women and song aplenty. Yes, he had done well in the wizard's service and had no desire to see that service end prematurely.

Magnus's expression gave no indication as to how he felt about the news. "And do we know what happened?"

"Well, Lord, because most of the kobolds were killed, it has been difficult to get solid information. As best as we can tell, it was a small group of treasure seekers that slew him. They wielded steel and magic beyond his ability to defeat and, after the battle, escaped unscathed. Our sources indicate that they have taken refuge with a tribe of mountain goblins."

The wizard smiled at the news, though it was not, in fact, news to him. He had known for some time that the ogre had been defeated and by whose hand it was done. It was Magnus himself, after all, who had given the order that the five be captured and brought to Crackrock's lair. He had hoped that they would be turned to his cause, but from the outset he knew that a battle between the adventurers and the ogre was far more likely than not. And if that happened...well victory by either side was acceptable.

The silence stretched uncomfortably, and after several minutes the servant hazarded speaking up again. "My Lord? Do you have any commands for me?"

Magnus looked down at his lackey, the smile still on his face. "Find out more about these 'treasure seekers' as you call them. Who are they? From where did they come? What do they want?" He paused a moment before finishing, "You have served me well. Now go."

"Yes, Your Wisdom," the servant replied then quickly climbed up from his knees and backed out of the audience chamber, head bowed the entire distance.

Magnus watched him go and took a sip of wine from the golden goblet on the table next to his throne. As it happened, he also knew the answers to the questions he had posed to the servant. The youths were from another realm, and almost certainly wanted to make their way back to it. More importantly, their quest to do so would eventually bring them to this very room. Plans fit together within his head; he moved them as if they were chess pieces on a board. He nodded slightly to himself in pleasure at how things were progressing.

"Captain!" he called out, and one of the pike-wielding soldiers snapped to attention and marched forward to stand directly in front of the throne. The ornately-costumed man gave a smart salute.

"Yes, Lord?" He stood at attention, eyes staring straight ahead. Because the throne sat upon a dais, this meant his gaze was focused on the wizard's shins.

"That man has served me well," he repeated. "Execute him."

CHAPTER 6

It's not that the cell wasn't cheery, as far as cells go. The straw heaped in the corner was relatively clean and appeared to even be free of bugs. There was a little window that allowed sunshine in. The "waste bucket" was emptied regularly. But it was still a cell, and no matter how you dress it up, it still isn't any fun to be inside one.

"So now what?" Allison asked, her voice still laced with anger. "Our cavalry is in here with us. Asleep, I might point out." She nodded at Chuck, who was curled up in the straw next to her, snoring peacefully. She gave his leg a kick and he startled awake.

"Hey! C'mon now. What was that for? Don't you know enough to sleep when you can?"

"Yeah well that was for your amazing work that got us all into the clink here. I thought you were supposed to be good at this. A real artist and stuff." The last she uttered in a mocking copycat of Cookie's voice.

Chuck shrugged. "Yeah well I was going on the

assumption that the original I was working from was legit. It's not my fault he lied to us about his being the real deal." He looked thoughtful for a moment. "Though I did think it looked a little funny, now that I think about it. And he seemed a little on the defensive side about it, too. So maybe it was my fault a little bit. Oh well. Isn't the first time I've been in a jail. You guys either, from what I recall." He let out a giggle.

"So, then what are we going to do? Just sit here?" She was clearly dissatisfied with his explanation.

"Well thanks to the fact that they only took our weapons, we'll have no problem making bail. It's not like we killed anyone, or stole anything. I have to wonder what Thaddeus was hauling in those wagons that made him want to bribe the gate guard. We were just hired muscle, though, and even if he was doing something not so nice, so long as we all hold to the truth we'll be fine. Which I have to say I find ironic given my line of work, but it is what it is. In the meanwhile, I'm going to try to get back to sleep because you never know when we'll be able to next. Wake me up if something important happens." The small man paused a moment and looked at Allison pointedly. "And your being grumpy isn't important." He then rolled back over and began snoring again.

"OK, fine." She rolled her eyes at him and slumped back against the wall, trying to take his advice. The others were all lost in thought and none made eye contact with her, so she didn't try to start any new conversations. At least she was taking it better than Stu, she consoled herself. Being locked in was clearly taking its toll on him. He paced back and forth like a caged animal. She allowed her tired eyes to close.

When Allison startled awake, the block of light on the wall shining in through the window had moved clear across the cell, suggesting that she had been asleep for some time. The others had followed suit; even Stu had given up his pacing and was laying peacefully. The grating sound of the key turning in the door woke the rest of them up, and by the time the door had opened, all five were standing warily, waiting for whatever was going to happen next. A young officer stuck his head in and with a bow of his head to Allison said, "Please come with me. His lordship will see you now." Behind him were several burly guards with pikes at the ready, their scowls suggesting it had been too long since they had used them last.

"His lordship," Jimmy said. "Sounds important. I wonder what that means."

The officer smiled and said, "Well it means one of two things. Either there is something special about you that his lordship wants to discuss personally," he paused, "or it means you're to be executed, since those sorts of orders don't come from the regular officers. And he likes to meet the condemned before they go to the axe. He says it reminds him that you… I mean they are real people getting the ol' chop chop." He seemed to remember himself all of a sudden and turned a bright shade of red. "But I'm sure it's the former, not the latter. The execution thing rarely happens."

"Lead on, MacDuff!" Chuck commanded imperiously, seemingly oblivious to the potential disaster awaiting them, and strutted through the door as if he was the one in charge. The others brushed the straw off themselves and followed along into the hallway. In total, there were five guards plus the young officer escorting them through the prison. Their cell was at the far end of the hallway, and as they neared the stairs they noticed another one holding Thaddeus and the rest of his caravan drivers. It was smaller than the one they had been in, had no window, and the straw looked like it had been there for years. Allison glared daggers at the older man through the bars, which he returned with a sheepish smile and a shrug. The difference the cells made the friends optimistic that perhaps there really was something special about them and they weren't destined for the headman's axe.

After climbing several sets of stairs and walking through what felt like miles of corridors, the friends finally arrived at a door with a single guard posted outside. On the walk they passed suits of armor, giggling ladies-in-waiting, and across the hall from where they stopped was a room where a portly older man gave a torrent of orders to what seemed like an unlimited number of stewards, maids, and other servants. The guard looked mostly ceremonial, wearing a uniform covered in medals that, while impressive, clearly wasn't designed for heavy combat. The blade on his halberd looked wickedly sharp though, so he obviously wasn't purely decorative. The man reminded Stu, whose family had taken a trip to Italy the year before, of the Papal Guard in Vatican City. After looking the group up and down and sharing a few quiet words with their escort, he banged on the door with the back of his fist, sending noise resonating through the hallway. At a muffled sound from within, the guard opened the door to admit the young officer, who announced, "I have brought them, Your Lordship."

"Excellent. Bring them in." The guards and the friends all piled into what turned out to be an office. The room was lit by several lamps hanging from wall sconces, augmented by a single, small window that cast a thin beam of light across the floor. On the two side walls hung battle standards, mounted swords, and other accoutrements of war, though the back wall was covered by a floor-to-ceiling bookcase, stuffed to near-bursting, suggesting the office's occupant to be more than just a military man. Behind an ornate desk constructed from polished oak sat a gray-haired man in an expensive looking military uniform. His suitcoat was immaculately tailored, making even the spit-and-polish guard outside his door look drab in comparison. The uniform was cut to show off the fact that despite the passage of years he was still in excellent physical condition. "Thank you, Alfred. You and your men are dismissed."

The young officer began to protest about leaving the prisoners alone with his superior, but the older man raised his hand to forestall the argument, looked over a pair of spectacles at them and let out a sigh. "I appreciate your vigilance, Alfred, but this office isn't big enough for this many bodies, and if they tried to put up a fight, none of your pikes would be worth anything in these close quarters. Please, take your men and go. If you feel like you must, you may wait with them out in the hall. Maybe you can take a look into the reports of those giant reptiles we've been hearing about. Or maybe even take a few days off. I honestly don't care where you go, but you can't stay here. My man Winston will be in the room with us." He raised his voice. "Winston, would you join us in here please, when there is finally some space?" The older man looked pointedly at Alfred with his last comment.

Alfred gave a dejected puppy look, then turned to lead his men outside into the hallway. Once they had exited, the man who had been standing outside entered the room and shut the door behind him. Facing the desk were two well-worn chairs placed upon a circular, woven rug.

The man took a few moments to arrange the papers scattered across his desk before looking up. "So," he began, pausing a moment to eye each of his prisoners up and down, pointedly not inviting any to sit. "My name is Count Cassius Hallowell, and I am the castellan here in Providence City. Because of my less-than-diplomatic nature," he indicated the weapons hanging on one of the walls with a scowl, "the more delicate parts of that role have been tasked to another, and I have the singular job of keeping this city safe and secure." He paused to take a sip of wine from the goblet at his elbow before continuing, "Specifically, what this means is that I have been given broad authority over the people here, particularly those who would cause our city harm. Even more specifically, what this means that I basically wield the power of life and death over anyone not rich, powerful, or well connected."

"Even more specifically," Chuck added, "us." He gave a courtly bow.

The man grimaced at being interrupted, but nodded and agreed, "Yes. You."

TJ cleared his throat, and Hallowell turned toward him with a raised eyebrow. The young wizard asked, "Well surely we aren't in a life-or-death situation, are we? We've never been here before, and while we admit that our papers were not necessarily in order, that hardly seems like something worth having this sort of discussion over. We don't need to stay here if we're not wanted."

The count leaned back in his chair, extending his arms up and back, clasping his fingers behind his head. "Well, there's the thing. Your papers are really the least of your worries. Your choice of traveling companions is the problem. The men you were with were involved in some serious criminal activities in the town of Hampshire, with which we have cordial relations. Extortion, murder," he ticked off on his fingers, "you name it. Those miscreants must have had an informant somewhere in the Hampshire Guard, because just before they were to be apprehended they packed up their wagons and fled this way. Hampshire hired some mercenaries to go after them and bring them to justice, but somehow, they eluded capture yet again." The friends exchanged glances, but none said a word.

"In the meanwhile, however, Hampshire had sent pigeons alerting us and other local towns that your friends were on the move and we should keep an eye out for them. It was only a matter of time before they showed up here or somewhere else and could be captured. And look who we captured right along with them." He stared down Chuck, who looked ready to chime in again. "Yes, you. Now your new friends are off to the axe man by week's end, that's for sure. But my conundrum is what to do with you. The easy solution would be to send you off to the chop as well and call it a day. Easy and profitable, from what the guards said you are carrying in your purses.

"But doing the easy thing isn't really my way, nor is it

the way to keep this city as safe as possible. Simply chopping the heads off of anyone who steps out of line is going to eventually result in a pretty small city. So, what do you think I should do with you?"

The five stared back at him in silence. After several long seconds Winston said, "I believe his lordship is asking for suggestions."

"Well," Jimmy offered, "could we just pay a fine and call it done? How much do you want? I'm sure we could cover it."

Chuck immediately winced at the suggestion, and Hallowell said, "I'm sorry, but are you attempting to bribe an official of Providence City? Did you hear that, Winston? I think they are trying to bribe me."

With a grim smile, his guard said, "Yes, my lord. I believe they are."

"So attempted bribery, in addition to forgery and aiding and abetting. That is hardly moving the scale in the correct direction." Allison paled at this, a fact that did not go unnoticed by the count. He waved his hand dismissively. "I already told you I could take all the money you've got and take your heads as well, so you're going to have to do better than that."

Stu, full of nervous energy from the time in the cell and visibly frustrated at the whole discussion, blurted out angrily, "Well if you aren't going to take bail money, what *do* you want us to do?"

Rather than returning the angry glare, the castellan's face grew bright, a wide smile creeping across his face. "Ahhhh," he began. "What do I want you to do, you ask? Now that is an interesting question." He tapped the side of his nose with his finger. "Because as it happens, there is something very particular that I want you to do. And if you do that very particular thing for me, we might be able to forget this entire unfortunate experience. If you are exceedingly successful, I might even arrange for you to get real papers, instead of those pieces of garbage you tried to foist off on us."

"Hey!" Chuck said, a wounded look on his face. "Those weren't garbage and you know it."

Hallowell shot the rogue a wink and continued, "So what do you think of my proposal? You do a favor for me, and I do a favor for you?"

"And the alternative is?" TJ asked.

"Unpleasant." The smile didn't disappear, but hardness crept into the count's eyes.

"Well, I guess we don't have much of a choice in the matter," he replied. "Though it would be kind of nice to know what it is you want us to do before we promise to do it. It seems to me we're already in plenty of trouble here. The last thing we need is to get involved in something else illegal." The wizard shot a glance at the castellan's assistant. "Or giant and reptilian."

"Oh, don't worry, my dear boy." The count's face voice lost its edge. "Lizards of unusual size? I don't think they exist. And I wouldn't dream of asking you to do anything that would smirch your spotless reputations. In fact, what you'll be doing may actually make heroes of all of us. Allow me to explain."

He stood up and paced while he spoke, losing himself in his words. "As I said, my job is the safety and security of this city. Of late, the safety and security of this city has been less than perfect. There has been a series of kidnappings over the last month or two, and we haven't been able to make any headway on the investigation. I've had my men scouring every inch of this city looking for evidence to help us find the missing people but have had no luck whatsoever.

"Now I'm sure you're wondering what the big deal is. Providence is a large city, and these sorts of things are going to happen. And that's true. We have kidnappings, burglaries, murders, what have you. But these disappearances have been different. First, the victims have not been the typical kidnapping targets. No wealthy heirs or heiresses, no merchants or members of the nobility. Instead, they have all been people like you. That is, mercenaries, soldiers, brawlers, toughs; the type of people who aren't worth the risk because they're going to fight back." He nodded at Jimmy. "For instance, if we hadn't had a dozen bowmen on the walls ready to turn you all into pincushions, I would have thought twice about trying to take your large friend into custody. That's not to say we couldn't have done it, but we would have buried more guardsmen than I would have liked. Yet these people have been plucked right off the street. Some even from taverns, surrounded by witnesses.

"The second difference is that as yet we haven't received a single ransom note. Zero. Zip. Zilch. What kind of kidnapper kidnaps people and doesn't ask for money? It just doesn't make any sense. As near as we can tell, the first abduction took place almost two months ago. I can understand letting loved ones sweat to increase ransom payments, but to not even let us know that they're alive?

That's crazy, or at least not the way that I'd go about doing it." He gave them a wink. "Not that I've ever kidnapped anyone, of course.

"So that gets you caught up. My own men have come up with nothing, despite searching nonstop for the last several weeks. That means one of two things." He held up his index finger. "Option one is that my men are incompetent. I've been doing this for quite a few years and I've never known them to be incompetent. Maybe a little overzealous like dear Alfred outside, but that's it." He extended a second finger. "Option two is that whoever is behind this is either influencing the investigation or has an informant in my organization and moves their operations whenever my agents get too close."

"So, what you're saying," Jimmy summed up, "is that you need some unknowns to look around and maybe find something that your own men can't because you have a mole somewhere?" He nodded with his head back toward the door. "That explains why you booted those other fellows out."

The castellan nodded and said, "Exactly. And, of course, you folks fit the profile of people being nabbed. As far as I'm concerned, worst case scenario, they make a grab for one of you. We've got a new lead, and the rest of you have a stronger incentive to finish the job."

"Speaking of which," asked TJ, "what's to keep us from just bolting out of town and your never seeing us again?"

"Half the innkeepers and all the beggars in this city are in my employ, and they'll be reporting back to me about your progress, or lack thereof. And, of course, the guards at all the gates will have your description by the time you have left the room, with strict orders to kill any of you who look like you're trying to leave the city. How's that work for you?"

TJ looked back and forth among his companions' blank faces. At last he said, "Well, I guess we've got a deal."

Hallowell and Winston both smiled. The five friends did not.

CHAPTER 7

Not long after their meeting with the castellan, the friends were back out on the street, evicted from jail with all their equipment returned to them. The guards who'd brought their gear to the count's office looked unconvinced as to the wisdom of rearming them, but followed their orders nevertheless. Now, the five stood near the entrance to one of the crowded market squares that dotted the city. Ribbons and banners in all the colors of the rainbow flashed in displays designed to catch the eye and draw customers' attention. The market stalls and booths carried a smattering of everything and food vendors were everywhere. The smells of dozens of different dishes wafted through the air, setting Jimmy's stomach rumbling. Allison elbowed him in the ribs, and said, "Are you ever not hungry?"

"When I'm eating!" He replied with a grin. He craned his neck left and right, taking in the sights. "So, what's the plan? Anyone have any ideas?"

Chuck said, "Well, I have a certain amount of experience with cities. I can poke around and see what I find in the back alleys and such. Though I almost wonder if we'd be better off doing the bait thing and waiting for something to jump out at us. I don't know how much I'll be able to find. I mean, if someone came out of nowhere and started poking around asking questions, I sure wouldn't be too sharing. And I can promise you the local thieves guild will be none too happy either. Could be a quick way to find myself floating face down in a river."

"How about those folks outside the gates?" Allison added. "I wonder if they've had anyone turn up missing. If so, maybe they'd be willing to share some information with us. Given their relationship with the town watch, it wouldn't surprise me if they were less than forthcoming with his lordship's men. We, on the other hand, are almost kindred spirits." She gave Jimmy another elbow.

"One thing is for sure," chimed in Stu. "Don't split the party. If you want to go rummaging around after dark, Chuckles, you do your thing. But we should otherwise all stay together. We've had too many close calls, and if even one of us is missing the next time we get jumped, things could get ugly quickly."

TJ nodded agreement. "Let's grab something to eat and see if there's any information to be had among the vendors. Once we're done with that, we can always head out to go check on those tent folks. We'll need to clear it with the count, anyway, so if we send a messenger now, by the time we're done eating we may have a reply." He asked Stu to bend over and scribbled out a message on a piece of parchment, using his friend's back as a table. Spotting a street urchin eyeing them warily, he motioned the scruffy-looking boy over and handed him a small coin with the note. "Take this to Lord Hallowell at the city watch, wait for a reply, and then return. If you do, I'll give you twice again as much. Three times as much if you're back within the hour."

"Yessir!" The child started off at a dead run, only to trip over Chuck's outstretched foot. The boy skidded head-first, arms outstretched, and before he could pull himself back up Chuck's boot landed on his back, pinning him to the ground.

"What are you doing, Chuck?" Allison exclaimed and looked around nervously for a member of the Watch. "We just got released! Don't you get us arrested again for assaulting children!"

Chuck rolled his eyes at his friend and helped the boy over to reach into his open tunic. He withdrew his hand to reveal a small leather pouch, which he threw to Stu. The woodsman was surprised to discover his purse of jewels. The young pickpocket had almost pulled off the score of a lifetime.

"Not much of a city boy, are ya, Stu?" Chuck gave a laugh, then turned serious as he turned his attention back to the urchin. "You, boy, will take that message just as my friend asked, and you'll be back in an hour. Otherwise I'll hunt you down and cut off your thumbs. Understand?"

Wide eyed, the thief nodded, then scrambled back to his feet and set off running again, this time in a different direction.

"His thumbs, Chuck? Really?" Allison scrunched her nose at the thought.

"Nah, I wouldn't really do that, at least not anymore." He paused a moment, lost in thought. "But for a boy in his line of work, just the threat is enough to set him on the straight and narrow for us. He'll be back in no time at all with our reply, and I bet he won't even ask for his money." His head jerked in a nod, as if he were satisfied with his assessment. "Now, let's go get some grub."

A nearby vendor was serving freshly roasted lamb across a plate-sized flatbread, sprinkled with herbs and a crumbly cheese, almost like a Greek Gyro, and it was the familiarity that unconsciously drew the five in. With all the strange things that they had experienced over the prior weeks, even the smallest reminders of home were comforting. The five passed the time munching on their food and discussing how to learn the information they needed, though they were unable to improve on their current plan. They were just finishing up the last of their meal when the pickpocket scampered up to them, out of breath and holding a sealed note marked with Hallowell's signet. Warily, Stu reached out to take it, keeping an eye on both the boy's hands, then thanked him and reached into his purse for a few more coins.

"Oh, no payment necessary, milord," the boy stuttered, hands raised. "Happy to be of service! I'll be going now! Be well!" He bobbed his head several times as he backed away, looking warily at Chuck's stern face. When he knew he was out of reach he turned and sprinted away.

"Told ya he wouldn't take the money," said Chuck, his mouth breaking into a grin.

"What does the note say?" Jimmy asked as Stu broke the seal and read through the writing.

"He says it's fine for us to go out there, but we should return by nightfall, and he will have people watching us. We can use this note as our pass in and out through the gates." He rolled his eyes. "Do we really have time for this distraction?"

"Don't see much choice," replied Allison. "They caught us red handed, after all. At least we're not still in that prison."

"Then I guess we should get a move on," he said with a sigh. "So, what did we decide, anyway? Shall we head out there today, or just poke around town a bit?"

Allison looked up at the sun, which had begun its descent toward the horizon. "Let's stay inside the walls for now. If we are expected back by nightfall, we'll probably run out of time before we're done out there. May as well find ourselves an inn to bed down in and set up a base of operations. Then we can do some more investigating from there." The others nodded agreement, and Allison asked the vendor at whose stall they had been eating to suggest a place to stay. The merchant gave them directions and the group set off to find their lodgings.

Their destination, the Dancing Unicorn, was only a few blocks away from the market square, and the walk was quick and uneventful. They had evidently impressed the vendor with either their clothes or the way Chuck had dealt with the pickpocket, because he had sent them to a relatively upscale establishment.

The building's facade was well maintained and there were small urns with flowers on either side of the entrance, a sturdy wooden door with iron clasps. Pushing through the door, they found the common room uncluttered and well lit. A small stage stood in the corner, just large enough for a few musicians to entertain during evening meals. A long bar stretched across the back of the room, behind which was a large, finely polished mirror. Surrounding the mirror were bottles of various liquors, and there was a hole in the wall through which a spigot protruded. Three long, low tables with benches were spaced out in the room, two of which were filled with well-dressed men and women sharing in low-voiced conversation.

The innkeeper, a fat balding man wearing a white apron, approached them immediately, eyeing them up and down as if trying to decide if they belonged in his establishment or not. His gaze lingered uncomfortably long on Stu, but when his eyes fell upon Allison, his demeanor suddenly changed, a large smile crossing his face. His eyes flicked to the side, where they made contact with those of a hulking brute of a man standing quietly to the side of the door.

The innkeeper gave a slight nod then spread his arms in welcome and bellowed in an accent that the friends somehow placed as 'southern,' "Welcome to the Dancing Unicorn, my lady, my gentlemen! My name is Habib, and I am honored to be your host." He bowed briefly before continuing, "Come in, come in, how may I serve you? You have found the finest inn in all of Providence City, and all that that entails. Please, sit down and let me bring you food and drink!" He gestured to the empty table and ushered them over, pulling a bench out for Allison to sit. The others in the room hardly spared a glance toward them, so this appeared to be his typical reaction to new guests.

"Juice if you have it," Allison began. "Mulled wine if

you don't," the others nodding their agreement with the request. She reached into her pouch and retrieved a gem at random, which turned out to be a ruby the size of her thumbnail. When she placed it on the table, Habib's smile somehow managed to get even bigger.

"But of course, my lady, my gentlemen. And to eat?" His head bobbed up and down like a bird, and his hand snaked out perhaps a little faster than necessary to take possession of the gem, which he immediately slid into an apron pocket.

"Nothing, thank you, we just ate," she replied. "But I'm sure we'll be here for dinner later, and we will need a suite of rooms if you have them available. At least two, preferably three." He nodded his head and bobbed several more times as he backed away, disappearing into the back room to fill their orders.

"You know, Allie," Chuck said with a grin, "that gem you just gave him was worth an entire month's profits for a place like this. I mean, it's not like we can't afford it, but we may want to be a little less open with our money. Even if we are trying to be the bait, we don't want the attention of every crook and criminal gang in town. There are some folks we really don't want to meet."

"Folks like you?" She stuck her tongue out at him, but his nod was serious.

"Folks much worse than me. Folks who really would have taken that boy's thumbs off without even thinking about it. I'd rather not take those sorts of chances, particularly when we're not on our own turf. Cities like this bring back memories I'd rather forget." He shivered.

"I agree," said TJ. "Let's lay low a bit and see what we

can find out. Maybe we won't need to attract anyone's attention."

Habib returned with the drinks and brought out a steaming loaf of bread and a bowl of butter, saying "Fresh from the oven, I thought you might like it even though you already ate. My Martha baked it, and it is the best you will ever have." He bowed again and backed away, leaving them to sip their drinks and munch on the loaf.

As the afternoon turned into evening, patrons came and went, and when it was time for dinner a young woman emerged from the back room to take a place on the little stage. Her dress and blouse were simple patterns in muted hues of green and blue, with only a trace of embroidery around the collar and cuffs. In her hand she carried a lute, and after a few last adjustments to the pegs she began to accompany herself in song. Although the locals in the room took much of the entertainment as nothing more than background noise, the five friends listened raptly. Some songs were about love, some about loss, and some were bawdy drinking songs, the words to which everyone else in the common room appeared to know.

Night came and Habib showed them to their rooms. It wasn't a suite per se, in that the rooms were not adjoining, but they had the three rooms at the end of the corridor to themselves. TJ looked anxious. "Are you sure you don't have anything with connecting doors? I'd feel much more comfortable if there was just a single door to the hallway for all of us."

The innkeeper looked at them with confusion. "A single door? Why?" Realization struck him and he put on a scandalized look. "Surely you do not fear for your safety, do you? I assure you that the Unicorn is plenty protected from street thugs by my own staff." His eyes narrowed as he weighed the money he had already been paid by Allison against possible damages to his inn if a serious fight broke out. "Do you expect trouble? I run a reputable business and want no trouble here. If you are that worried, you should take your business elsewhere. I can recommend some establishments that might be more to your preferences."

Allison raised her hands in a placating manner. "No, no, we are new here in town, and don't expect anything like that. We've just had a difficult couple of weeks and are still a little on edge. You will have no trouble from us, and no trouble should come looking for us." Her eyes met his and she held his gaze for several seconds before he finally nodded his acceptance.

"Very well. Please let me know if anything is not to your liking or if there is anything I can do to make your stay more pleasant. You may break your fast as early as an hour before sunrise if you are so inclined." His voice turned softer. "The streets of Providence City are not safe in the wee hours of the morning in the best of times, and recently there have been rumors of even darker dangers. After midnight, the door is locked and barred, and you may not go out or come in. Please plan accordingly. Grant, whom you saw at the door earlier, sleeps in the common room with his cudgel while his big brother keeps watch during the evening."

"Big brother? Good grief, how much bigger is he?" Chuck shook his head in disbelief.

"Substantially," replied Habib with a grin. "As I said,

we are plenty protected. You will have no troubles this night." Looking back to Allison, he continued, "If my lady would like a bath before bed, or in the morning when you wake, please let me know, and I will have my daughter draw you one. This room here," he gestured to the center door, "has a tub and we need only fill it with water." The size of her grin was all the reply he needed. He nodded. "I'll have it drawn directly. If any of you gentlemen would care for a bath, we can have a tub moved into your room, or you can use the one at the other end of the hallway. Do you have any questions for me, or last requests before turning in for the night?"

Faced with shaking heads, he gave them another of his bob-bows and retreated down the stairs. Stu muttered, "Last requests, huh? I'm not sure I like his choice of words there," to which the others nodded their agreement. "Can we trust him?"

All eyes looked to Chuck, the least trustworthy of the group, who gave a slight sigh. "It wouldn't surprise me if dear Habib is in the half of this city's innkeepers that are on Hallowell's payroll. Or if he isn't already, he will be by the end of the night." He paused and considered. "But can we trust him not to slit our throats in our sleep, or let someone in to do so? Mostly. This is a nice enough place that word of midnight stabbings would do a number on his business."

"Only mostly trust him not to slit our throats?" Stu sounded uncertain. "That's not the vote of confidence I was hoping for."

"Give me enough money to retire to some distant land in extravagant wealth, and I'll slit all your throats, myself," he replied dryly. After a few moments he added more sheepishly, "In a matter of speaking, of course. We're already extravagantly wealthy."

Rolling her eyes at Chuck, Allison said, "Well I, for one, am going to take advantage of that tub," and danced into the room Habib had indicated as hers, closing and loudly bolting the door behind her.

"Well, how about TJ and I take one room and you two take the other," suggested Jimmy. He patted the wizard on the back before continuing, "He's the squishiest, so just in case something does end up happening, I should probably be near him. You guys can take care of yourselves well enough without needing me standing between you and the folks with the pointy things."

With no one disagreeing, they split up into their respective rooms. Jimmy placed his sword next to his bed, slipped a dagger under the pillow, lay down, and was asleep within moments. TJ watched with amusement at how easily his friend could turn himself off. Quietly opening the door, he stepped back out into the hallway, where he uttered a short incantation. If anyone approached their end of the hall the ward he set would wake him immediately. Just because Habib believed in his inn's security, it didn't mean that TJ had to. He retreated to his room and lay down on his bed, entering the meditative state he used to refresh his magical powers each evening. Within minutes, a claxon in his head jolted him upright. He shook Jimmy wake and hurried to the door. The larger man slid open the peep hole and peeked out, only to relax when he discovered the disturbance was only a young woman carrying two pails of water into Allison's room for her bath.

"False alarm," Jimmy muttered before returning to his bed and collapsing back into sleep. Satisfied that his wards were working and that all was indeed well out in the hallway, TJ also returned to his bed. The alarm went off several more times in the following minutes, but he dismissed them all with a thought.

Across the hallway, Stu and Chuck were sitting on their beds looking at each other. "So, the door is locked and barred, huh," Stu said to Chuck with a grin, doing his best Habib impression. "And we may not go out or come in."

"That's what they tell me," returned Chuck.

Together, they approached the window and looked out. The view down to the cobbles below was unobstructed by trees, and oil lamps every fifty feet or so provided ample lighting for the street. In the distance they could hear a Watch patrol marching their rounds. To the two boys it seemed like a peaceful night in a peaceful part of town. In spite of this, the few pedestrians out and about moved quickly from lamppost to lamppost, as if afraid that any errant shadows might snatch them away into the night. Given what the group had been tasked to do by Count Hallowell, perhaps that fear wasn't entirely unfounded. After a quick glance at Stu, Chuck turned the window's catch, slid the glass upward, and climbed onto the sill. One hand holding onto the inside pane, he leaned out to look upwards, and was pleased to note that the roof was only a half dozen feet away. His eyes found the imperfections in the wall's masonry and he used them to scurry up the short distance to the roof.

Stu, his bedroll strapped across his back, followed a moment later, having jumped the distance rather than climbed it. The roof, like all the others in this part of town, were flat instead of gabled, with several chimneys breaking through. He spread out the bedroll and lay down, gazing up at the stars and relishing the breeze that drifted across the rooftops. The smells of the city were much different than the smells of the outdoors, but by breathing through his mouth and closing his eyes, he could almost imagine himself out among the trees he had come to love so much.

"You gonna zonk up here tonight?" Chuck looked at his friend amusedly and hunkered down next to where he lay.

Stu put a finger to his lips and replied, "Shhhhh," a smile across his face.

"Suit yourself. That means I get my pick of beds. I'll be back later. I've got some work to do."

At this, Stu roused himself. "You're not going to go steal anything, are you?"

"Of course not!" Chuck said in a mock-offended voice, his hand over his heart. "I would never steal anything!"

"No, really." The humor was gone from his voice. "Are you going to get us in even more trouble than we're already in? 'Cause the sooner we can get out of this awful city the happier I'll be. The wilderness is calling to me, Chuckles. I used to think I spent the first fifteen years of my life living in an apartment building." He took a breath. "But now I think maybe I spent that time sharing a cottage with one of the King's foresters and his wife. I don't belong here amid the brick stone. And one thing is for sure, I'm not going back to that cage they put us in. If you get us thrown back into prison because you can't keep your hands to yourself, it'll be the last mistake you make."

"No, really, I'm not. I promise." Chuck sighed, letting the none-too-veiled threat pass without comment. "I can't say I'm not tempted, though. I'm just as conflicted as you. I can feel that same pull on me, drawing me into the backstory I wrote for myself. It gets harder every day, too."

"Exactly. My whole family all hated the one camping trip we went on a couple years ago. And the first year or so of these gaming weekends I went home each night to sleep. And yet here I am lying on a roof when there's a nice cozy bed six feet beneath me. This stinks. I want to go home and sleep in a bed and take a bath and never wear leather again." After a moment he added, "But then again, I don't. Right now there's nothing I want more than to be under a tree somewhere next to a campfire. And nothing I want less than a featherbed."

All Chuck could say was, "Yeah."

The pair sat in silence for several long minutes, each lost in their own thoughts, before the little man stood up and said softly, "OK, I'm off. Sleep well. I'll be good." He jogged to the edge of the inn's roof and leapt quietly to the building next door, disappearing into the night along the Rogue's Highway.

CHAPTER 8

Chuck paused on a rooftop to allow bypassers below to move out of earshot. So far, the night had been unproductive. As Chuck had expected, the locals were not particularly forthcoming to an outsider. He knew a few people were holding back information he could have used, but he'd decided not to push them too hard. As it was, he was taking a risk using the rooftops to get around. He might have been mistaken for a burglar, and thieves' guilds were typically very territorial. The last thing he and his friends needed was both the city watch *and* the underworld unhappy with them.

Eventually he had been directed to an information dealer willing to speak with him. Of course, there was a difference between being willing to speak with him and actually telling him something useful. In exchange for the gem Chuck offered the man he received only vague accusations about the newcomers outside the city and what was essentially little better than fortune teller's mumbo jumbo about sewers, dark wizardry, and the like. Even before the man had stopped talking Chuck knew he had wasted his money.

Back up on the Thieves' Highway, when Chuck approached the inn, he discovered a figure standing on the roof. At first he assumed that Stu must be having trouble sleeping. Perhaps he had trouble ignoring the city sounds and smells after all. When he got closer, however, he noticed a second figure squatting next to Stu's prone body. Dropping to a crouch, Chuck paused to squint to make sure that neither of the figures was one of his friends. Once certain, he pulled one of his daggers from its sheath on his sleeve and threw it at the figure standing up. Although he would have preferred to take his time, possibly using his blow gun and poison, he didn't know if Stu was even still alive, and any delay could make the difference between life and death for his friend.

The blade flashed across the distance, lodging itself in the man's shoulder. He gave a grunt, raised a crossbow, and fired in Chuck's direction. The hastily aimed shot flew wide. Chuck vaulted across the gap to the inn's roof, and when he was close enough to feel confident that he wouldn't hit Stu's prone form he hurled a dagger at the second foe. The figure jumped backward and the dagger embedded itself in the wood with a loud *thunk*.

The two men ran and jumped to the next roof. Chuck took off after them, another throwing knife in his hand, but before he himself could jump, an arrow fired from across the street hit him in the thigh. His knee gave out and he collapsed, skidding to a stop just before the drop to the ground below. A second arrow narrowly missed his head and he scrambled to get behind the inn's chimney. He yanked the arrow from his leg, nearly blacking out from the pain, then tore off a piece of his shirt to use as a makeshift bandage. Peeking around the corner, only his lightning reflexes allowed him to avoid a third arrow aimed directly at his head.

Chuck crawled around the chimney, favoring his injured leg, but when he looked around the corner he was unable to spot the sniper. He tore off a second piece of cloth from his shirt and draped it loosely over the tip of the arrow he'd pulled from his leg. He peeked again, this time extending the tip of the arrow past the chimney's front corner. As expected, another arrow flew towards his ruse and he was able to trace its trajectory back to its source. There, he could just see the archer crouched in the shadows on the roof directly across the street.

Happy he had thought to bring all of his tools with him, Chuck opened a hidden pocket in his cloak and retrieved the small case that carried his blowgun, needles, and an assortment of poisons. He carefully assembled the blowgun, then withdrew a needle and a vial of viscous liquid. This was the perfect time, he decided, to try the one he had received from Finkelbert and the Bonecrushers. It would knock the archer out quickly, and then when he regained consciousness he could be interrogated to find out just what he was up to. With a little bit of luck, this would be exactly the lead they were looking for. Chuck applied the poison and slipped the needle into the tube. Once again, he leaned out around the corner of the chimney and slowly brought the weapon to his lips. The archer wasn't where he had been a few moments before, and an agonizing minute later Chuck had still not managed to find him in the shadows. Before giving up completely, he tried the fabric on the arrow trick again. But having successfully protected his associates' retreat, the archer had fled into the night.

Chuck placed his blowgun and pouch on the ground limped over to the motionless body of his friend. Stu's hands and feet were bound, and a burlap sack was tied around his head. The subtle rise and fall of his chest indicated he was still alive and breathing, and Chuck, who only then realized he had been holding his own breath, let out a sigh of relief. He quickly removed the sack from over his friend's head, then untied the knots and lightly slapped Stu's cheeks.

"Hey Stu? Stu? Can you hear me, buddy?" When neither the slapping nor the sound elicited any reaction Chuck sat back on his heels to consider his next move. He was confident that the assailants were long gone, but still didn't like the idea of leaving Stu lying there exposed. He padded lightly to the edge of the building and leaned over to look down on Allison's window. The room was dark and there was no sign of movement. Further, the window was shut tight, which he hoped meant that no one had tried to abduct her during the night as well. He crossed to where Jimmy and TJ's window faced out. It was also closed and dark, but he had run out of options. He reached to a lanyard at his side that held a blackjack—a small wooden club perfect for knocking people unconscious with a single whack to the back of their head. With a quick flick, he arced the weapon toward the window, which shattered loudly.

Noises came from below as the two men in the room scrambled out of their beds to prepare for an assault. Chuck quickly called down to them, "TJ! Jimmy! Stu's up here and someone was trying to kidnap him. Get Allie up and get her up here. I can't wake him up!" Jimmy's head poked out of the window and looked up.

"OK, TJ's going to her door now. There a stairway? How are we getting up there?"

Cursing, Chuck looked around anxiously for a trap door leading below. He soon found one, and discovered it was bolted from the inside. Chuck quickly counted the steps from the trap door to Jimmy's window and relayed the information down, hoping that it didn't open to another patron's room. Not more than a minute later the door opened upward, followed immediately by the large berserker, his sword drawn. Only when Jimmy was satisfied that there wasn't a trap did he call down to Allison to join them on the roof. Their healer dashed up, a lantern in hand, and ran over to where Stu lay. Allison set the lantern next to him and inspected his body for any obvious signs of injury. TJ stayed below to make sure no one tried to surprise them from inside the inn.

"I already did that. There's nothing I can see," Chuck pointed out impatiently.

She waved her hand at him in dismissal and continued her work. "Aha. Here." A tiny feathered barb poked out from his pants leg, which she plucked out and showed to Chuck. "You do your thing, I'll do mine." She gave it a sniff and wrinkled her nose, then handed it to the rogue. "What do you think? Foxglove?"

Abashed at not having found the needle himself, he

took it from her humbly and smelled it as well. He gave a quick nod and replied, "Yup, that's it. Looks like they just wanted to knock him out for the trip to wherever it is they were taking him. No permanent damage, and only a mild headache when he regains consciousness. Not so easy to get, but easy to apply, and little risk of poisoning yourself by accident."

Jimmy growled. "What was he doing up here anyway? Idiot. I know we were planning on doing the bait thing, but I kind of figured we would talk about it first and come up with a plan to capture someone for information. If this was the one shot they were planning on taking at us, we totally blew it." His eyes narrowed as he looked at Chuck. "And what were you doing out here too?"

Allison shook her head and said, "We'll worry about that later. Let's get him back downstairs and into a room and we can talk about all this when he wakes up. I should be able to speed up the process a bit, and maybe take the edge off his headache." She motioned to Jimmy to take Stu's shoulders and she grabbed hold of his ankles. The large man sheathed his sword and moved to comply, but before they lifted him Allison cocked her head to the side like a confused dog, then looked at Chuck. "You're injured too, aren't you? Where? Let me see." In the darkness she hadn't seen Chuck's bloody leg, but now that the panic over Stu had passed she could sense it from where she was standing.

"I'm ok, really. It's not so bad." Allison sat him down nonetheless and unwrapped the makeshift bandage. The wound looked clean and she gave it a sniff to make sure that it hadn't been poisoned as well. If it had, the effects would almost certainly have already set in, but better safe than sorry. Convinced that it was just a simple puncture, she placed her hand over it and channeled her healing power into his leg. In moments the wound had closed, and he was bending his knee as if he had never been struck. "Can't help with the pants though," she added, smiling. "You're going to have to replace those yourself."

"Thanks, Allie. I really appreciate it." The look on Chuck's face suggested he was surprised that she had taken the trouble to heal him, and she noticed it right away. Despite his having saved the others from the kobold's lair, he still felt guilty about ditching them the day that Simon was killed.

"No sweat. That's what friends are for. 'K?" Her eyes held his until he nodded his head, then she turned back to where Jimmy was waiting. "OK, let's get him back downstairs and into bed and I'll try to wake him up."

TJ looked anxiously from below, and as Allison and Jimmy descended with Stu, they discovered Habib's shape filling the doorway to the small storage room that held the stairs. "What is going on up here? What are you doing in my closet and on my roof? Someone said they heard glass breaking!" He was in a dressing gown and breathing heavily, as if he had jumped out of bed and immediately run upstairs. He did not look happy.

Allison handed Stu's feet to TJ and approached the innkeeper. Turning on all the majesty she could muster and hoping that her magic ring would help her pull it off, she declared, "We heard noises on the roof, and while your men are guarding the door, there are obviously other ways to get in. We went to investigate, and you can see what happened." She nodded to where the boys were carrying Stu and pointed at the bloody hole in Chuck's pants. "Your inn is now safe. For tonight. You are lucky we were here." The force of her words and the fire in her eyes made Habib's bluster disappear and he returned to the head-bobbing from earlier in the day.

"Of course, my lady. Thank you, my lady. I am indeed grateful for your assistance. Please, is there anything I can get you?"

It was still too early for breakfast to have been started, and she didn't really want to push her luck, so she just smiled and said, "You are welcome, Habib. And no, there is nothing we need now, other than the quiet of our rooms to nurse our companions back to health, but thank you for offering."

He looked grateful to be let off so easily and head bobbed himself back down the stairs. Unsurprisingly, none of the other guests had peeked out of their doors, though they were undoubtedly all wide awake and holding their breaths. The four marched down the hallway into Allison's room. There, they bolted the door, lay Stu on a bed, and placed an extra blanket over the window to completely dampen out any shadows that might be visible through the curtain. Allison applied her healing magic to the spot where Stu had been shot, and then traced her hands up his leg, beginning at the wound and moving toward his heart, neutralizing the poison as she went.

Stu's eyes opened with a jerk and he sat straight up in bed. "Oh! Hi guys! What did I miss? And why am I in Allie's room?"

CHAPTER 9

Needless to say, no one got any more sleep that night. Instead, they stayed up talking about what to do next and shot furtive glances at the window. Surprisingly, Stu was the least bothered by the entire affair, though perhaps that was because he was still feeling the aftereffects of the poison that had knocked him unconscious. He lay in Allison's bed, his back propped with pillows, his fingers clasped behind his head.

"Ok, so what's done is done. I shouldn't have been up on the roof in the first place, I know. But I couldn't help it." He shrugged. "Chances are I'll do it again tomorrow night if we're still here."

"Or still alive," muttered TJ.

"Or that." Stu nodded. "So instead we have to figure out what to do next. Tonight they came hunting for us. Now it's our turn." His eyes met Chuck's and a flash of understanding passed between them. The hunt was something they both understood, even if they hunted on two completely different types of terrain. "We're going to need more information. Real information, instead of that junk about sewers and dark magic." Chuck nodded.

"OK," said TJ, still irritated about Stu and Chuck being outside overnight when he thought they were safe in their own rooms. "Where do we look for information? The locals don't seem interested in talking to Chuck, and you can bet they're not going to be any more willing to talk to the rest of us. The Watch has no idea. Our best bet was dangling out some bait and then trying to ambush the kidnappers, but I'd be willing to bet that between last night's fun on the roof and Chuck's making the rounds asking about them, they're not going to want to be anywhere near us. What's left to do?" He asked in exasperation.

After a moment's silence, Allison spoke up. "Well, if the locals won't talk to us, maybe we should look to the non-locals. We were already planning on checking out the folks in that tent city, I say we keep with the plan. Maybe they'll have had some of their own people turn up missing and will have begun their own investigations. Or, at the very least, they will have made some better contacts here in the city that we can get some real information from."

"But what if they're involved in the kidnappings?" Jimmy looked unsure about the plan. "Didn't one of the people Chuck talked to last night suggest that they were involved?"

The rogue shook his head. "I seriously doubt it, based on how they've been described to us. If these folks are horsemen and tent dwellers, they're not going to be the types to jump from rooftop to rooftop. And if it were really them, I'd have gotten a much different response from the information sellers last night. I didn't learn much, but what I did is pointing towards the bad guys being a local gang, or at least having some strong local backing."

Jimmy seemed satisfied with this explanation and nodded his head. "Good enough for me."

TJ looked like he still wanted to argue, but realized that there wasn't anything left to argue about. Stu was right. What's done was done. The best they could do was move forward and hope they got a lead somehow. He sighed. "OK. The sun is starting to come up. Let's go downstairs and get some breakfast, and maybe some coffee. Then we can head out to the tents and see what we can find. If worse comes to worst, I guess we can go back doing the Scooby Doo thing and bait a trap."

"Oh yeah. Breakfast. That sounds like a win to me!" A wide grin on his face, Jimmy stood up from his chair and crossed to the door. He looked at his massive sword propped against the wall, and after a moment's hesitation took it and slung it over his shoulder. "It may only be breakfast, but I'm not being caught flat footed again." No one could find fault with his logic, so they all took their weapons with them as they left the room and headed for the common room.

Downstairs had a much more subdued feel to it than it had the night before. The same cheery fire burned in the hearth, and the smells of bacon and fresh bread wafted from the kitchen, but it was obvious that people were on edge. Faces mixed with fear and hostility turned toward the friends as they entered, and virtually all conversation ceased. Habib hurried from behind the counter to greet them.

"Ahh, my friends, good morning! I trust the rest of your night was undisturbed? These sorts of occurrences are rare at the Unicorn, I can assure you. I, and the rest of the guests, are grateful for your assistance and protection from whatever it was that made that mischief last night. Isn't that right, my friends?" He turned to face the others already breakfasting there. The looks on the other patrons' faces said the exact opposite, that were it not for the five, that sort of mischief would never have happened. Not having gotten the backup he expected, some of his animation faded and he stuttered, trying to pick his train of thought back up. "Anyways, please, come and break your fast. Do you have business to attend to today?" His voice implied he was hoping that once they finished said business they would be on their way and he could forget the whole experience.

"Yes," TJ announced, understanding immediately. "We do have some business to attend to today. With luck we will wrap it up within several days. And then, much as we appreciate your hospitality, we will have to move on to our next destination." Habib's face radiated gratitude and he visibly restrained himself from hugging the wizard. The mood in the common room lightened somewhat as well, and a smattering of conversation returned. The group continued to receive nasty looks from the others every so often however.

The innkeeper led them to a table, then hurried to bring them large plates of the food they had smelled when they first came down, as well as a decanter of freshly squeezed orange juice. The five dug into their meals with gusto. There was way too much for Allison, but the boys stabbed at pieces of her food with forks until her plate was clean as well. When the last crumbs were gone they stood up and said thanks to Habib for the food. Allison smiled. "We should be back later today, but if for some reason we aren't, feel free to close and lock the door on us. We'll be OK out there."

As they walked through the door, they had to pass Grant, who stood impassively at his post, staring straight ahead. Jimmy patted him on the shoulder and murmured, "Don't worry, we'll be gone soon enough." The enormous bouncer let out a low growl and his eyebrows furrowed, but otherwise he didn't move.

Once out in the street, Allison asked her large friend, "Did you have to do that? It's not like last night was his fault or anything. Guy's just trying to make a living, you know."

Jimmy grinned sheepishly. "Yeah, I know. But something in me made me say it anyway. I guess snarkiness and ale drinking are some of my own character traits peeking out. And, of course, massive strength." He flexed his biceps in a classic bodybuilder's pose.

"Not that I'm really one to talk, but you probably ought to try to bury that a bit," said Stu. "We've already got plenty of enemies. We don't need to add to the list."

Jimmy rolled his eyes. "Yeah, yeah, yeah. So which way are we headed?"

Everyone looked to Chuck, who had spent the night exploring the city. "This way," he replied, pointing to their left. "We go about six or seven blocks, hang a right, and we'll bump right into the gate that's closest to where the tenters are set up. Ten-minute walk, tops." He looked up at the sky and squinted. "Might be a wee bit early, yet. Do you want to do any shopping before we head out? There are a couple markets within a spitting distance of where we are, though in the dark it was hard to tell what they were selling."

Jimmy gave Chuck's arm a friendly punch. "You mean you didn't break in to any of them?"

Chuck actually blushed, before mumbling something unintelligible as he rubbed his arm.

TJ broke the awkward silence by saying, "No, I think we're all good. Let's not delay this any longer than we have to. I'm already sick to death of this town, and I want to get out of it as soon as possible. Yanno?" Stu nodded wholeheartedly.

"I hear ya," replied Chuck. "Was just offering. So, let's get a move on."

The city began to come alive as they walked, with shopkeepers opening their windows and doors and residents dumping their waste out of windows. More than once it was only Chuck's quick reflexes that kept one of them from having something smelly dumped on top of them from above. After the third time, they decided to walk down the middle of the road rather than along the sidewalks, even if it meant they then had to dodge carts. To all their minds, being trampled by a horse was far superior to having night filth in their hair.

As Chuck promised, it was not a long walk to the gate, and when it came into sight, the party stopped to eyeball it. It was much smaller than the one through which they had come with the caravan: this one was barely wide enough for a single cart, and virtually everyone who was going through it was on foot. The security seemed just as strict here, though, with guards checking papers of everyone as they passed through.

The people in this part of town appeared quite a bit different than those of the day before. There was a lot more leather and much less cotton, on both the men and women. These men tended to sport full beards, whereas in the other parts of the city men went clean shaven, perhaps with slight mustaches. And everyone had a dagger or a sword, or even both, strapped to their sides. It was clear that many were visiting from the tents outside.

"Well, let's do this." TJ eyed the bowmen atop of the wall, just as many facing in towards the city as looking out. "And let's hope this note works for us." They moved together in a clump toward the gate guards, pulling together unconsciously into a defensive ball. They all knew that if it came to a fight, they were easy targets for the archers like that, but they also wanted to feel each other's nearness.

This early in the day the wait was slight, and when they got to the gate TJ handed the guard the note from Hallowell. The sentry gave it a quick scan and nodded, then handed it back and said, "I was told you might be coming through here. Keep an eye on your valuables and don't stay out past dark. Those savages haven't caused us much trouble yet, but I know they're planning something." He looked left and right conspiratorially and gave Jimmy a disapproving frown. "It's only a matter of time before something explodes, and you five don't want to be out there when it happens. OK?"

"Yes sir, we'll remember that. Thank you, sir. Have a good day, sir." TJ took the note back from the guard's outstretched hand and tucked it inside his shirt, then found himself giving the same little bob-bow that Habib had been using since they first arrived at the Unicorn. The guard looked at him with a raised eyebrow and a shrug before turning to the next person in line. The friends hurried through the gate, looking up at the walls and back over their shoulder as if they expected to be turned into pin cushions at any moment.

Though Stu looked visibly relieved at being outside the city and back in the fresh flowing air, it was only after they were comfortably out of bowshot that the others relaxed. They followed the road for a few hundred yards before brightly colored fabrics floating in the air indicated that they were getting close to their destination. Occasionally the group passed a tenter heading the other way, toward the city. Bearded, armored and armed, they were clearly a different sort of person than the typical city dweller.

They soon began to hear the sounds and smell the smells of the giant tent city. Small pens housed sheep and goats and children sat watching their little miniature flocks. Although none of the little ones looked to be older than ten or twelve, they were all armed with a dagger and a bow–it was clear that the newcomers were just as wary of the Providencers as the city dwellers were of them. The shepherds looked at the friends warily, unsure of what to make of these people coming from the city but clearly not city dwellers. Allison was surprised to note that the aura of majesty her ring projected appeared to have no effect on them. She didn't think this was the time to ask TJ about it but made a mental note to do so later. "The gate guard was right," she murmured to Jimmy, who walked at her side. "This is an explosion just waiting to happen." The big man nodded.

Just past the livestock pens the tent city began in earnest, even boasting its own version of gate guards. Rather than a uniform tabard with identical pieces of armor, the men and women standing watch seemed to be wearing whatever they could throw together. Two wore mail shirts and coifs, but most wore an assortment of leather pieces, giving them the appearance of having been conscripted to stand watch. When called to serve they simply came in whatever they had handy.

The five approached the sentries, who immediately moved to block their path. As the friends pulled up short, TJ moved to speak, but Stu placed a hand on his shoulder and stepped forward to be directly front of the foremost guard. The man looked Stu up and down, mentally putting pieces together, then locked eyes with him, staring impassively. The pair remained this way for about a minute, until the guard suddenly moved to strike, his arm flashing upward toward Stu's face. In a flash, Jimmy drew his sword, and two daggers appeared in Chuck's hands. Stu, for his part, remained completely still, and the guard's hand stopped just shy of his jaw. The guard's face split into a grin, and he stepped back saying, "You are welcome here, brother. Your friends, however," he nodded toward where Jimmy and Chuck still looked ready for a fight, "could use a little lesson on etiquette." During the entire exchange the other guards hadn't moved a muscle, even when blades had been drawn.

Stu released an overly dramatic sigh. "Yes, I know. But they're city folk, if you know what I mean." He gave the sentry a nod before saying, "Thank you." At the term "city folk" all of the tent dwellers chuckled in understanding, then stepped aside to let the five pass. Chuck and Jimmy had sheathed their weapons, but as they walked between the guards, the pair eyed them warily. The guards, in contrast, ignored them as they passed, looking toward the city and sharing some gossip about the goings on in the camp.

Once they had gotten out of earshot, TJ asked, "What the heck was that about? And how did you know to do that?"

"Don't ask me," Stu answered. "It just seemed like the right thing to do. I wouldn't go so far as to say these are my people–they're probably more Jimmy's people than mine —but their lifestyle seems to be much more like what I'm used to. These aren't the type of people to want to see paperwork and travel passes. They want to know that you're not going in to cause trouble and that you aren't hot headed." He looked back at the other two boys. "You two almost blew it, but I guess they were willing to let you in 'cause you're with me." He stopped and turned abruptly, the other four almost walking right into him. Looking at them each in the eyes in turn, he said, "Don't draw your weapons in here again. This is an armed camp, even if it doesn't look like it. There'll be no fighting our way out of this, no matter how hard we try. OK?"

"You got it." Jimmy nodded his understanding.

Chuck shrugged and said, "I'll do my best. But reflexes are reflexes, and I'd rather step on someone's toes than be dead." That seemed to be sufficient for Stu, who continued to lead the way further into the encampment.

The caravan leader/criminal Thaddeus's description of the tent city fell well short of the reality. Although everyone lived in tents, this was no temporary settlement. It had everything one would expect from a permanent town. Merchants of all sorts had set up their shops and hawked their wares at anyone who made eye contact. The nearby ringing of metal on metal provided evidence of a blacksmith hard at work nearby. The spacing of the tents suggested some sort of city planning, with wide thoroughfares and smaller side streets. None were cobbled, of course, but the dirt had been packed hard by continuous travel.

Looking around, Allison said, "OK. We're here. Now what? Those folks we met out front didn't seem very chatty. How are we supposed to get any information out of these people?"

Chuck shrugged and said, "Don't look at me. I'm out of my element here. I'm thinking this is Stu's and Jimmy's party now. Maybe they can make some friends."

They all turned to look at the ranger, who suggested that they start wandering. "They don't look organized enough to have a formal watch we could check in with, so we're probably better off *making friends*, as you put it. Maybe we can find a tavern or something. We aren't going to make any progress out here in the street."

Stu turned and began walking. The others exchanged looks, surprised at how much Stu was talking, compared to his normal, taciturn self. He seemed much more comfortable here than in the city's streets, or the goblin's fort before that. Allison wondered, not for the first time, if he would stay with them to the end of their quest, or just disappear into the wilderness someday.

No specific destination in mind, they just began to move "inward," hoping to find denser population and something approaching a commons or a tavern. One thing was for sure: wherever they walked, heads turned. Inside Providence City the leather-wearing tenters seemed to be the oddballs, whereas here the five friends stood out like sore thumbs. Even Stu, with his clean-shaven face, attracted stares. To their minds, someone carrying himself as a woodsman was expected to have a man's beard. TJ, for his part, appeared to be viewed with outright disdain. At least once they overheard a none-too-subtle comment about men who wear dresses, and there were several more derogatory comments about magic and the types of people who use it.

"Geez," TJ complained. What's that about?"

"Well up in the north where I grew up," answered Jimmy, "magic wasn't particularly accepted. It wasn't viewed as especially manly. You see, real men whack at each other with large pieces of metal until one person or the other falls over." He shrugged and added, almost as an afterthought, "Or both. Even archery was considered a coward's way of fighting. No offense, Stu. Add to that, we are a simple people with pretty simple thoughts. Magic is a tricky thing for most people to get their minds around, and you know what they say: you fear what you don't understand, and you hate what you fear." Grinning from ear to ear, he concluded, "The long and the short of it is that I wouldn't expect anyone to treat you as anything more than a little girl."

TJ sighed. "Barbarians."

"Not barbarians, berserkers!" Jimmy corrected. "There aren't any barbarians in this game world." He chuckled and even TJ cracked a smile. "Anyway, my own run-ins with magic before I met up with you folks were not particularly enjoyable." The large man shook his head as if to free himself of an unpleasant memory.

"OK, fair enough," TJ replied. "I'll be sure to keep out of the way. So long as they don't expect me to whack anyone with a large piece of metal. I never took any weapon skills at all, so I'd probably just cut my own legs off if I tried."

Just as they finished talking they encountered another group of men headed the opposite direction, laughing loudly at some joke and clapping each other on the back. Stu, in the lead, moved over to the side of the road to let them pass. Although Allison and Chuck followed suit, TJ and Jimmy, who had been looking at each other as they talked, didn't move quite quickly enough. TJ's shoulder brushed against one of the locals.

The man staggered backwards as if he had been hit by a moose running at full steam, his arms flailing around. His feet slipped out from under him and landed in the dirt on his backside, as if he were a soccer player taking a fall to cause a penalty call. "OY," he roared. "What was that for?"

TJ looked around frantically, wondering if there was someone else nearby who had actually hit the man. Seeing no one, he simply stared, mouth agape, as the man picked himself up and dusted the back of his pants off. His friends were laughing at him, and his face had turned the color of a ripe tomato. "Wow, he sent you flying, Eddie!" "Need us to get you a cart?" "You fall over easier than my two-legged goat!"

Eddie took two long strides to stand directly in front of TJ. "What was that all about? This road belong to you or something?"

TJ looked uncertain, and his friends were frozen in their tracks. "I, uh, um..." was the best he could do.

The angry man stepped a little bit closer and continued loudly, "How much of this road do you need? My buddies and I even moved over to the side to let you all pass. Being good hosts to visitors, you know." He turned to look at his friends, who nodded agreement and encouragement.

TJ looked over at his own friends, unsure of what to do. "Um, I'm sorry. I wasn't paying attention, and I didn't mean to knock you down."

This seemed to be exactly the wrong thing to say. If it was possible for Eddie's face to get any redder, it did. "You mean you weren't even trying to knock me down? Is that what you're saying? That you don't even need to *try* to knock me on my arse?" This elicited another round of catcalls and hoots from his friends.

TJ looked desperate. "I said I'm sorry. Please. What can I do to make it up to you?"

At this, Eddie gave a wicked grin. "Oh, I know exactly what you can do." He cracked his knuckles. TJ, uncertain, took a step back.

In a blur, Jimmy's fist slammed into the side of Eddie's

head. The struck man's eyes rolled back into his head and he collapsed like a sack of potatoes. As everyone else in the street looked on, completely stunned, Jimmy unclasped the baldric that kept his sword attached to his back and released the clasp. "Shall we?" He inquired. His eyes burned with madness and he flashed a wicked grin of his own.

Chaos ensued. The five other tenters leapt forward with a roar, fists flying wildly. Three immediately ganged up on Jimmy, pummeling his face and body with multiple blows, though they seemed completely ineffectual against his bulk. He flailed back at them but was unable to land any additional knockout blows of his own.

Chuck and Stu both stepped forward to meet the attack, while TJ shrank backwards against one of the tents, next to where Allison stood clenching and unclenching her firsts as she watched the melee unfold. She began to murmur under her breath, reciting an incantation she had learned from one of the Bonecrusher healers. While it was not as impressive as TJ's haste spell, her friends grew a little bit stronger, and a little bit more resistant to the blows they were taking.

To Jimmy's left Stu had entered a boxing stance and was bobbing back and forth, his fist snaking out when an opportunity appeared. His opponent had entered a similar stance, and was giving as good as he got. It was not long before both men's noses were leaking blood and one of Stu's eyes had closed. The other brute's face had also taken a beating, and his bottom lip had swollen to twice its normal size.

On the other side Chuck faced off against a man easily

twice his size. The giant tenter swung his arms wildly in arcing blows, any one of which would have knocked Chuck senseless were it to land. However, years growing up and performing activities of questionable ethics on the streets had honed Chuck's reflexes into near superhuman levels, so try as the larger man might, he was unable to connect. Allison could see the brute's frustration level increase with each missed swing and could tell that Chuck had begun to play with him, not taking the fight as seriously as he should. She hoped that it was confidence, and not overconfidence, that motivated him.

Meanwhile, in the center of the street, Jimmy stood off against his three opponents. One dove low at him, hoping to trap his legs and topple him to the ground so his friends could pile on top and pin him down. Jimmy had in fact been waiting for just such a move, and he brought his knee up just in time to meet his opponent's chin. A nasty crack split the air as the man's jaw broke, and he fell to the ground, writhing in pain. At the same time, another of the men had jumped toward his chest, and while Jimmy hadn't been expecting that, he was still able to get his guard up and keep himself from being bear hugged and dragged downward. The third circled around Jimmy, but rather than press the big man, he turned, nodded his head to Allison with a, "Ma'am," and his hand flashed out, landing squarely on the bridge of TJ's nose. The shocked wizard collapsed in a heap and Allison let out a little squeak.

TJ's assailant returned his attention to Jimmy, who was still fending off the one grappling him from the front. He kicked Jimmy right in the kidney, eliciting a grunt of pain from the berserker. As he wound up for a second kick

Allison jumped on top of his back with a loud whoop and wrapped her arms tightly around his neck. Surprised, his arms flailed about wildly as he tried to get a grip on her, and in moments his brain, deprived of oxygen, shut itself of and he fell to the ground, Allison on top of him. As she landed, her shoulder slammed into the packed dirt and she felt something give. Instinctively the pain made her roll off her shoulder, but unfortunately she rolled into the back of Jimmy's legs, which buckled from the unexpected force. He fell backwards, the other man on top of him, and as he landed their heads slammed against each other, stunning all three.

Chuck was still holding his own, dodging back and forth to avoid the swings. Because of his shorter reach, however, he hadn't landed any shots of his own. On a whim, as the other guy's hand passed over his ducked head, he danced in to land a punch to the belly. Pain shot up his arm and into his shoulder, as if he had punched a steel plate rather than the light leather jerkin. He stepped back, shaking his wrist ruefully as the other man smiled down at him before taking another swing. Changing strategy, Chuck sprung in again, this time his punch directed right between the legs. This, he discovered, was a much more tender area. The big man let out a horrible noise and doubled over. Emboldened, Chuck stopped to observe his handiwork. This was a costly mistake, for one large fist flew out and caught him right in the breadbasket, knocking the wind out of him and sending him to the ground wheezing. After this one retaliatory strike the man fell over on top of Chuck.

Stu and his opponent were still going at it, both so

bruised and bloody they looked more like they were slow dancing than fighting, each propping himself up with the other. Tied up on each other's shoulders and striking feebly at each other, they both noticed the lack of sound at the same time. As one they turned their heads to survey the scene, and found everyone else on the ground, out of commission. Again making eye contact, each took a few half-hearted swings at each other before Stu's knees finally gave out from exhaustion. His opponent, having been using him as a crutch, followed him to the ground, where they both lay panting.

The silence was finally broken by a cheer erupting all sides. Turning their heads, they saw a crowd had gathered, and looked to have even been making wagers on the fight. This, for some reason, struck Stu as funny, and he began to chuckle. The man next to him began as well, and it wasn't long before both were sobbing with laughter, coughing blood every so often as they tried to catch their breath.

"So, you new in town?" The other man asked between laughs.

"Yeah. That gonna be a problem?"

"Nope. I think you'll fit right in."

It was at that point that Stu lost consciousness.

CHAPTER 10

Allison had been busy. Not that anything was particularly hard to heal—well, the broken jaw was, and she wasn't sure if the guy with the concussion would ever pronounce his letter "S" normally again—but there was a ton of little things to be seen to. Stu and his partner, whose name was Bill, were bruised messes, even after the healing. They claimed to feel better, but the giant purple blotches across their faces told a different tale. Chuck seemed to be okay, and she was really glad there hadn't been any major damage to his opponent, not really relishing the idea of trying to concentrate healing in that particular area. The others all had split eyes or puffy lips or wretched headaches, and she had to use every bit of her power to make everyone feel better. TJ and the fight's instigator, Eddie, she left with their pounding heads. Served them right for starting the whole mess, she thought.

After Stu and Bill had finally fallen to the ground (and

all the bets had been settled), the spectators had stepped in to help get things sorted out and cleaned up. This meant fetching bandages for the folks who were bleeding and buckets of water for those who had passed out. When they had uncovered Chuck from beneath the bruiser, the first thing he had said was that Allison was a healer, so hers was the first head they dunked. Once she had completely come to, she had gone to work.

The last big role that the spectators filled was the one of refreshment provider. Even before everyone had been woken up and patched up, jugs of ale were being passed around to all the combatants. Jimmy jumped right into it, as did Stu. If anything, the brawl had made them feel more at home out in the tents. Allison shook her head when the jug came her way, not wanting the drink to interfere with her ability to work. Chuck, having had years of living off his wits and his reflexes, politely took the offered drinks but either handed them to Jimmy to drink, or dumped them out when no one was looking. TJ, a sour look on his face, had several glasses, in the hopes that the alcohol would numb the pain shooting through his head.

"I still don't understand what that was all about," he muttered. "If all you wanted to do was hit the bars with us, you could have just asked us outright."

Eddie, sitting next to him and swilling his own ale for the exact same reason, replied, "Nah, we couldn't do that. Don't you have standards for whom you drink with? We wouldn't be seen with anyone who didn't know how to fight. And since we'd never seen you in a fight, this is the only way we could know. I mean, you're wearing a dress, and all, you know." He paused a moment and then said with a mischievous grin, "Of course, we had no intention of drinking with the lot of you. We'd planned on giving you a good drubbing and then heading off on our own. But here we are," he said and raised his mug in salute. "And since we're here, let's have another!" He clinked his mug against TJ's, and the two of them drained their drinks.

At last everyone was patched up, or as patched up as they were going to be, and the group of tenters got up to leave. "Thanks for the fun, fellas. And lady," Eddie said. "Maybe we'll bump into you again some time." This caused them to break out into laughter as they started to move on.

"Wait!" Stu called out. They stopped and turned, looking curiously. "We're actually here looking for some help, and so far you're the first people we've really met." He rubbed his sore chin and added ruefully, "I'm kind of hoping you'll be the only people we meet, but that's another story. We came out here on a whim, looking for some information, and we don't really know where to turn. Maybe you guys could help us out?"

The locals exchanged glances and shrugs, then Eddie said, "Yeah, sure. I don't see why not. Let's go find somewhere to sit that's not the middle of the road and we can chat. Maybe we can be of help to you. It is the least we can do after the bit of fun you gave us."

"Yeah. Fun," Allison muttered under her breath.

The two groups walked for about five minutes up and down a number of streets before settling on a large tent with its flaps rolled up. Inside looked very much like any tavern you would find inside a brick and mortar city. There were tables, a bar, a small stage where a musician or two could stand, and it was horribly lit. As they all sat down, a barmaid arrived with mugs for everyone and waited patiently to be paid. "We got this," Stu said, "since this was our idea." He reached into his pouch and withdrew one of the smallest gems he could find, then placed it in the woman's hand and closed her fingers over it. He figured they were again overpaying, and while he didn't expect it to remain a secret for long, he didn't want to flaunt it in front of their new friends. She smiled and curtseyed and returned to the bar, emitting a little squeak when she saw what was in her hand.

"I'm thinking we need to hit a money changer," whispered Jimmy to TJ, who nodded in agreement.

"Don't the taverns ever ask you what you want to drink before they serve you?" Allison was looking at the mug of ale in front of her with distaste. The healing she had done had given her a splitting headache and the last thing she wanted was the bitter, sour drink this promised to be.

"Well, I guess they *could* ask," said Bill, "but seeing as they only have one item for sale, there wouldn't be much point, huh?" Seeing the friends' looks of confusion, he continued, "Where we're from, we don't have buildings with cellars filled with all sorts of drinks. Because we never know when we'll have to pack up and move to the next spot, it doesn't make sense to have a large selection. Most taverns specialize in one particular drink, and people go to the one whose drink they prefer. When we come here, we know exactly what we're going to get."

"Like McDonalds, huh?" Chuck said. This time it was the tenters' turn to look confused, so he added, "Oh, never mind, inside joke."

Mug in hand, Eddie got down to business. "So, what is it that you need the People's help with? Can't promise anything, but you seem like decent folks."

Stu opened his mouth to speak but Chuck cut him off. "The People? That's what you call yourselves?"

Eddie looked mildly amused by the question and several of his friends let out a chuckle. "Of course that's what we call ourselves. You have to understand that for most of our history we roamed wildlands uninhabited by anyone other than animals and monstrous humanoids like orcs and kobolds. We were the only *people* there. How else would we refer to ourselves?"

After a moment's thought, Chuck nodded his head. "Fair enough."

"OK," said Stu, casting an irritated look at the rogue. "Now don't hold this against us, but we have been," he coughed and looked sideways at his friends, "encouraged to do some freelance investigation work for the city watch." He saw the change in their hosts' demeanor and quickly continued. "No, it's not what you think. We're not here to do anything to you or your people. It's something else entirely. We just don't have any leads, and we thought maybe we might be able to find some information to help us out here."

Eddie's face had hardened at the mention of the Watch, but he didn't seem ready to get up and walk out yet. He looked around at the faces of his friends before finally saying, "All right, we're listening. Go on."

"So there have been kidnappings, and the victims are people who aren't normally the targets of kidnapping. People like you and me, fighting types. And the weird thing is that there's never any ransom note, or any sign of the victims. The Watch has turned up no leads whatsoever, and we got roped into helping them. And by roped, I mean blackmailed."

"And so, you came out here because you think one of us is behind it?" Eddie spat. The conversation didn't really seem to be going in the right direction. "That's not really how we operate out here. We got a beef with someone, we take 'em head on in the light of day." The look on his face suggested he was thinking about going another round with them out on the street. The others of the People looked like they might take it further and draw steel.

Chuck jumped in to try to help save the sinking ship. "No, exactly the opposite. We know that you're not involved. Or at least pretty sure," he added with a shrug. "Stu here almost got nabbed last night. If I hadn't been prowling about looking for information and gotten back to the inn at just the time I did, he would have been gone, and we would never have known where. The thing is, those folks weren't like you. The way they jumped from roof to roof. They knocked Stu out with a poison made from foxglove, which I'm pretty sure isn't your style. One of them was really pretty handy with a bow, too. None of it points to anyone from out here."

"OK, so then why are you even here?" Bill was looking impatient, though Chuck's explanation seemed to have smoothed down the ruffled feathers.

"Well, we're new in town. Actually just got in a few

days ago. So, it's been tough finding any information. No one really wanted to talk to me, or at least talk to me seriously. Maybe if I were in my home turf I'd be able to get people to open up, but people seem more scared of *them* than they are of me, so they're all clammed up.

"Now, the way we figure it, you're new in town, too. We thought that maybe if any of you had heard anything about what is going on, you'd be willing to help us out. For all we know, you may have been losing some of your own people and begun your own investigation. All we are looking for is a lead to get us in the right direction."

The tenters exchanged looks before Eddie finally said, "Yeah, we've heard things. A couple people went missing. Only a few, but they were not the type to go running away so we know something happened to them. We hadn't heard that it was going on in the city, too. In fact, we figured it was the folks inside the city who were doing it to us, trying to frighten us away from here or something. That's why we posted those sentries at the entrance to our camp. They're not really going to keep anyone from coming in who really wants to, and they certainly aren't going to repel an attack. But they're keeping an eye out for anything out of the ordinary. Such as you, for instance. It wasn't exactly coincidence that we ran into each other back there. Word spreads quickly here.

"But do we have any leads? Not that I've heard. If we knew anything, we would have already acted on it." His companions nodded their agreement of this assessment, and the friends' hearts fell at the thought that they probably were not going to learn anything of value.

TJ looked at the others in resignation. "So, what's our

next move, since this seems to have dead-ended? We don't have any leads in town either, so I guess we just go back to Hallowell and tell him we failed and see what happens. I don't expect it will be a pleasant chat."

"Well, we could just make a run for it," chimed in Chuck. "We're already out here and we've got plenty of cash so it's not like we need to go back and get our stuff. That's what I'd be doing if it were just me."

The wizard shook his head. "No, my spell book is back at the inn, and that's not something I can easily replace. I doubt we're going to find any wizards around here at all, let alone ones who would be willing to scribe me a new book." He gestured toward the other patrons in the tavern.

"Oh yeah, forgot about that part. Well, the rest of us could make a run for it…" He looked thoughtful.

"*Chuck!*" Allison interjected. "That's not funny, even if you were joking." They all hoped he was joking.

Everyone sat quietly for a few minutes, each in their own thoughts about what to do next. Eventually, Eddie broke the silence. "Well while you're here, how about we show you around. There's going to be a Challenge today. Those are always interesting to watch. Normally they're not for the public, but you can be our guests."

"A what?" Allison asked.

"A Challenge. Someone is making a challenge for the position of warlord, the leader of our group. If someone believes that the current warlord isn't doing his job well, or is getting too old to lead, they challenge him to single combat in front of everyone. If the challenger wins, they become the new warlord. If not, the current one retains his title and his leadership."

"That seems like an odd way of succession. I bet the poor guy must be facing off challenges every other day, every time someone disagrees with a decision."

Eddie shook his head. "Well actually, not really. It is a fight to the death, so you really have to want to take control, and you really have to think you can win before you make a challenge. Most people are content to stop at simply complaining about things, rather than stepping up to try to fight, so they're pretty rare. We've gone as long as ten years between Challenges in the past, but it's only been a year since the last one. That's what makes this so interesting."

"Wow, that's a quick turnaround. Why the fight today?" Asked Jimmy.

"Some folks are less than pleased about the fact that we have been camped here for the past several months. In my lifetime we have rarely stayed in the same place for more than a month before packing up and moving on to new grazing and hunting grounds. Our current warlord claims that this is temporary and once things in the East have settled down, one way or the other, we will go back to our traditional way of life. Others, however, believe that he is trying to make us soft like the city people. No offense intended, of course."

"The East?" Allison inserted. "What does the Arcanum have to do with your people? Isn't the whole point of your traditional way of life so that you can just up and move to where the grass is greener?"

The tenter shook his head. "Normally you'd be right. This kingdom wants to fight that kingdom? Sure, go at it." He knocked his fists together for emphasis. "We'll just spend a few years in another part of our grazing area and come back when you've beaten each other bloody. Maybe sack a town or two while we're at it." He winked at Jimmy. "But this is different, and everyone knows it. When Magnus finally moves west, there won't be anywhere to go. North, South, he'll have control of it all. We're here because we know that if there's going to be any sort of resistance to his attack, it'll need to be unified, and it'll be centered here. The only question is whether or not these city dwellers have the spine to fight back, or if they'll just roll over and join up."

"Not that it'll make a lot of difference," Bill muttered. "If the fight gets this far west we're all gonna die anyway."

Eddie clapped him on the back with a laugh. "You're almost certainly right, my friend. But at least we'll die in glorious battle!" He raised his mug, and the other tenters followed suit. After a loud cheer they drained their drinks and slammed the empty mugs on the table. The tenters, focused on their drinks, missed the worried looks that shot from face to face among the friends.

"Well what do you guys think about the change in lifestyle?"

Eddie shrugged. "Putting aside the whole issue with the Arcanum, I'm happy either way. Of course, I'm young enough that change doesn't really bother me, unlike like some of our kin. The life of a nomad was good. Always plenty of fresh meat and the opportunity to mix it up with some of the humanoid tribes that cross our path every so often. And for some of us, that is what life is all about. But I can't deny the fact that I like not having to pack up everything I own and move every several weeks. That gets tiresome. And having a city nearby with all of its advantages is awfully nice as well. When we travel we might go half a year between cities, stopping only long enough to trade the pelts we have hunted for metal and other objects we can't easily produce ourselves." The others at the table nodded in agreement.

"So the new guy wants to you all to pack up and move back out?" Allison asked. "And everyone will say, 'OK,' and that will be that? Everyone will pack up and move back out?"

"Well yeah," replied Eddie. "How's that much different from the way you city folks live? Your king tells you to do something and everyone gets up and does it, and that's that. We're the same way, except we change kings a little bit more often."

She continued to press. "So what if a big brute of a guy, who happens to be an idiot, takes over and starts making bad decisions for you all? If no one can beat him, you could be following some meathead for years."

"Again, I ask how that's any different from your kings." He winked and everyone at the table laughed.

"Touché,' she replied, conceding the point.

"And in fact, custom dictates the warlord to be at least thirty years of age, to make sure that whoever holds the position has had a certain amount of life experience and isn't just some hotheaded angsty teenager." He drained the last of his drink. "Anyway, it should be just about time for the show to start, so let's go see what we can see. Hopefully all the good seats won't already be taken." His friends all chuckled at this, and they stood up to leave.

"Thanks for the drinks," called Jimmy as they headed out of the tent and back into the sunlight.

"Any time," came the barmaid's excited reply. "Really, any time!" She waved enthusiastically.

CHAPTER 11

The tenters led them through another series of turns before they finally arrived at an enormous tent, easily the size of a football field. There was something of a crowd outside, and they heard some voices talking about how the tent was full. Eddie, however, led them right past the people standing around, and when they got to the tent's "door" said, "They're all with me." The man barring the way for everyone else nodded his head and ushered them in.

Jimmy elbowed TJ. "First time making past the velvet rope outside the club, huh? We're moving up!"

Allison's assessment that the tent was the size of a football field seemed right on target. There were makeshift bleachers all along the perimeter, giving it a stadium feel. The only thing missing, she thought, were popcorn vendors. Four tall poles supported the tent's roof and were spaced out to provide plenty of room for combatants to move. Eddie took them directly across the center of the tent to an area that had been roped off, half its seats unfilled. "There ought to be room for us all," he said, and then plunked himself down right in the middle of the first row.

"Wow, nice seats," commented Chuck, who had also situated himself in the front row. "How did you manage to score these tickets?"

Eddie looked confused for a moment, trying to parse Chuck's words, before finally saying, "Oh, if you mean why do we get to sit here, well it's because it's my father that's the warlord. At least for now."

"*Woah*," Jimmy exclaimed. "Your dad is the boss, and he's about to fight some guy who hates him to the death? You sure are awful calm about the whole thing."

"Well, my old man can handle himself. Certainly better than I could handle your fist!" He chuckled. "I know the guy who is challenging him, and I don't think he has much chance of winning. My dad is stronger and been in more fights than him. I'd be shocked if this lasted long at all. And you have to remember, this isn't a case of two guys who hate each other going at it, but rather two people who have different visions for how our people should live. It's nothing personal at all. In fact, the challenger is my uncle."

"You have *got* to be kidding me," said Allison. "It's like the Lion King or something. This is just too weird."

"Weird to you is normal to us. And the last lions around here were killed by hunters decades ago. Now watch, it looks like things are about to get started."

A hush had come over the spectators as two men entered from opposite ends of the tent. Even from a distance, the family relationship was clearly evident in their faces. There looked to be about five years' age difference between the two, though both were still young and healthy. The older one was armored in the same leather that most of the people in the tent city seemed to favor. He also carried in his hands a sword about the same size as Jimmy's. As he walked across the dirt floor he gave the blade a few slashes, as if to loosen up his wrists. His face was full of determination and his eyes never left his brother's face.

The younger one appeared much less imposing, and looked to be about a head shorter than his brother, though he carried himself with confidence. Instead of the traditional leathers, he wore a mix of plate and chain. A solid looking breastplate was strapped across his chest, embossed with a dragon motif. Metal bracers covered his forearms and greaves covered his legs with chain on his shoulders and biceps, and down his legs beneath the greaves. A chain coif protected his head. In his right hand he carried a long slim blade that seemed designed for piercing rather than slashing and in his left hand was a long dagger with an oversized crossguard.

"Who is who?" Whispered Chuck.

"My father is the younger one," Eddie whispered back. In retrospect, it was obvious. The older, traditionally armed man was the one fighting to protect what he saw as their way of life, whereas the younger man, open to new ideas, was armored in a newer style, and his choice of weapons was more appropriate for a city dueler than a charging berserker.

The two men met in the middle of the arena and eyed

each other briefly before embracing. The challenger uttered some words too soft for the audience to hear, but when the warlord shook his head, a sad look on his face, it was clear the older man had asked him to change his decision and thereby avoid the fight. Some words from the warlord, presumably asking his brother to withdraw the challenge, were also met with a headshake. The two men looked at each other a moment more before taking a few steps back and raising their guards. The fight was about to begin.

They began by circling to the right, getting the feel of the ground beneath them and looking for possible weak spots in the other's defense. The challenger struck first, leaping forward with surprising speed, the point of his giant sword aimed straight for his brother's heart. A loud clang resounded through the tent as the parrying dagger came up and caught the blade in its guard, twisting and turning it away. The rapier snaked out and were it not for the fact that the deflection had knocked the challenger off balance the fight would have ended then and there, for the tip of the blade slashed right across where the man's throat had been but a moment before. The warlord danced backwards, his brother turning to regain his balance and reset his guard.

Allison, eyes not leaving the melee, wondered aloud, "How is he holding off that giant sword with just those little ones?"

Jimmy replied, "It's not always about the size of the blade, but how you use it." At her sideways glance he added, "What part of their sword you parry and what part of yours you parry with makes all the difference. Physics will jack you up in sword fighting." When her look didn't change he continued, "No, really. It's all about angles and fulcrums and stuff."

Again, they eyed each other warily. Eddie's father had the shorter reach of the two, so as his brother moved forward, he danced backwards or to the side, occasionally swatting at the larger sword with his own, smaller one. Again, the challenger sprung forward and again the parrying dagger flew up, but the larger man had put more muscle into the thrust this time, and the deflection was not complete. The point of the sword hit the breastplate just under and to the side of where the warlord's ribs were. The point skittered sideways across the metal, leaving a deep scratch as it travelled. The contact put the smaller man off balance, making him unable to repeat his counter-attack. He staggered backwards, trying to regain his footing.

"See that?" Eddie said in a hushed voice. Despite his earlier nonchalance, he was sitting on the edge of the bench, fists clenched and shoulders tensed. The crowd within the tent was dead silent, held rapt by the gravity of the combat. "If my father had been wearing the same leather my uncle has, or even mail, that sword would have sliced right through and it would be all over. This is one of the things my father has been trying to impress on our people. Holding onto traditions for the sake of tradition is not always the best idea, especially if changing something can improve your survivability out in the world." After a moment he added, "I hope that whichever way this goes, the rest of our people understand that."

As he spoke, his uncle followed up his stab with a series

of strong, double handed slashes. The warlord continued to stumble, not having caught his balance. Even so, he deflected the first with his sword, and then the second. On the third, the older brother spun a full circle to increase the momentum and strength of his swing. As the rapier came up again to parry, the heavier sword sliced the weapon in half rather than being deflected. The warlord looked at his useless sword in dismay and cast it aside. The challenger took another step, and another spin, and swung the sword again with a roar. As one, the crowd leaned forward, as if eager to get a closer look at the killing blow, and Eddie's knuckles were white where they gripped the bench. At the last moment, the warlord raised his parrying dagger to block, and while it indeed turned the attack aside, the strength of the swing knocked the blade from his hand and sent the People's leader tumbling to the ground, weaponless.

"That's physics, too," Jimmy murmured to no one in particular.

As his older brother approached him, sword held high, he crab-walked backwards, delaying the end as long as possible. And yet his face didn't show fear of death, or even resignation. It continued to radiate the confidence with which he had entered the tent. The challenger stopped just short of his brother's feet and looked down for a moment, sword still raised. Though no sound reached the friends, it seemed that they were exchanging words again, perhaps an apology for how things were going to end.

At last, the older brother prepared for the swing that would end the Challenge and return their people to their nomadic ways. As he stepped forward to deliver the killing blow, the warlord clicked his heels together and kicked upwards towards his brother. To those watching, it seemed futile, and almost petty. He had lost, and whether or not he managed to land a kick to the groin, the sword was going to do its thing. In even that last insult, the strike appeared to fail, falling several inches short, connecting instead with his brother's upper thigh.

The challenger paused a moment, then collapsed to the ground. It was only then that it became clear that a blade extended from the toe of the Warlord's boot and the kick had driven it through his brother's femoral artery. The quick blood loss caused the challenger to fall unconscious within seconds, and he was dead soon after. Many in the crowd leapt to their feet, cheering wildly, Eddie and his friends among them, though it was clear not everyone was pleased. It looked like the brothers had the support of two very different factions.

The warlord stood up slowly, stiff from the fight. He looked down at his brother and shook his head sadly before retrieving the other man's giant sword from where it lay. With one strong swing he brought the blade down across his brother's neck, severing his head from his shoulders. He then drove the blade point first into the ground and walked over to where Eddie stood without a single look back. As he walked, several other men entered the arena and approached the body.

The foursome looked markedly different from most of the others the friends had seen since arriving at the tent city. Rather than leather armor they wore untreated hides, some with patches of fur still attached. Tattoos decorated every inch of their exposed skin, including their faces and even their ears, and each walked with a staff from which an assortment of bones, teeth and shells hung.

Once the four had surrounded the corpse they began a ritual chant and in moments the body turned to dust. A sudden breeze passed through the tent, scattering the dust across the ground until it was no longer distinguishable from the rest of the dirt. By the time the warlord had sat down next to his son with a groan, the chanters had once again retreated to the side and all evidence of his brother had vanished. All evidence except for the sword planted in the ground, almost as a grave marker.

"Whoa," said an awestruck Jimmy, who stood to shake the Warlord's hand. "That was totally awesome!" He could hardly contain the excitement in his voice.

"That was my older brother, and my best friend," replied the Warlord in a monotone. Despite his apparent stoicism, he was clearly upset by what had just happened.

"Oh. Um. Right." Jimmy had the good grace to look abashed as he retook his seat.

"Is there going to be another challenge today, Father?"

The warlord looked at his son and said, "Yes, there is going to be a challenge for a captaincy. I believe for the Groundhogs." He looked over to where an assistant had approached and raised an eyebrow. The man bowed before him.

"Yes, Excellency. It is indeed the captaincy of the Groundhogs for which the challenge was issued." The warlord again stood, then the two stepped a few paces aside to confer in private.

"Wait a minute," said Allison, holding her hands out in protest. "OK, I can kinda get the martial combat thing for the person in charge of the whole shebang, though I've got to say that disintegration thing was kind of creepy, but you people kill each other over an officer position? Is it really worth it? How do you manage to have anyone left to do the actual fighting? Whatever happened to annual performance reviews and promoting people? That's what they do at my folks' law firm."

"For anyone to assume a leadership role among our people, they must prove themselves in battle." Eddie explained after the briefest look of confusion. "We are a martial people, and so we cannot afford to have someone who can't fight giving orders, even if for only a single company. However, as you rightly point out, we can't have people killing each other every time they want to move up the hierarchy, so we produced a solution.

"Years ago, some of our most powerful mystics worked together to create an artifact of wonder. By weaving their powers of healing and alteration together, they infused the artifact with the ability to make combat non-lethal. That is, I could stab you, and you would feel the pain, but rather than bleeding to death, your wound would close by tapping into your body's internal energy. What this allowed us to do," he concluded, "is continue to allow trial by combat without the messy side effect of all those extra corpses."

"It doesn't seem like it worked so well just a few minutes ago," Chuck pointed out dryly.

"Well that is an exception to the rule. As I said back at the tavern, the idea behind challenges for the warlord position was to make it appealing only to people who felt strongly enough to put their very lives on the line. If there were no permanent consequences, we would be in the situation you described earlier: all my father would do is fight off challengers, day in and day out. So, the artifact doesn't work when there is a challenge for the warlord position. In fact, we go in the other direction for those—the disintegration of the body ensures that there is no possibility of the dead being raised through healing magic." His eyes roamed over to where his uncle had lain. "But for all other challenges, losing isn't permanent, just very painful."

"This whole thing is just so totally bizarre," said Allison. "I think I'm going to step outside for some fresh air. I don't need to see another round of gladiator battles. You boys and your constant fighting." She stood up, made an awkward bow/curtsey towards the amused-looking Warlord, who had just rejoined them, and slipped out through the back of the tent.

"She does have a point, you know," the older man said softly. "You'd think there would be a better way to determine who is best to lead than have people whack each other into submission. Or death." He looked sadly toward the sword in the center of the tent, then shook his head. "Of course, that was how I got this job in the first place, so who am I to say anything?"

"Aw, c'mon," Eddie said in an attempt to break his father out of his melancholy. "I know you like a good brawl as much as anyone. In fact, that's how we met our new friends. This big guy," he slapped Jimmy on the shoulder, "dropped me like a sack of potatoes. I missed the entire fight!" His friends all laughed, and the warlord's face did crack a smile at the image.

After a moment he turned serious again. "Ok, settle down, boys. It looks like the next match is about to start."

At that very moment, two figures followed the same path the warlord and his brother had taken only a few minutes before. They were both considerably younger, neither long out of their teens. One's beard had not yet grown in, and neither of them had the bulk evident on many of the older men in the arena. "Good grief," murmured Jimmy. "I bet I could take both of them at the same time. And they're going to duel to the mock-death?" One of Eddie's entourage hushed him.

It appeared that both had fully embraced the new warlord's worldview. They each had sword and parrying dagger in their hands rather than the large sword favored by the late challenger. They also wore the combination of mail and plate that decreased mobility but enhanced protection. Perhaps most importantly, they each turned to salute the stands where the warlord sat before turning back to each other. It was a clear demonstration of support following the earlier Challenge.

It was only after a few moments that the friends realized that the beardless one was actually a young woman. "Wait. She's going to fight him?" TJ asked Eddie.

"If she wants to be captain, she is." Eddie replied, amused. "Does that surprise you?"

TJ had no reply, so Jimmy supplied, "The best swordsman I've ever fought was a swordswoman. She beat me almost every time, back when we were training." I'd think twice about challenging her to a duel, for sure.

Stu nodded in agreement. "I've known some deadly women, too."

Finding himself outnumbered, TJ only managed a, "Huh," in response.

The pair of youngsters also engaged in some talking back and forth, though it was clear that they were acting more from ritual rather than any desire to actually avert the fight. When both had finished saying their bit, they began to circle. In many ways it seemed anticlimactic after the duel for the warlord's position. Neither had the grace or power exhibited in the first battle, and when they began swinging at one another it became clear that they lacked the skill as well.

The man swung at the woman first, and she easily blocked the blow with a loud clang. She then counterattacked with her own slash, which was also deflected, and they both backed off. This pattern repeated itself several times with the same result. After the third pass Jimmy let out a groan and began providing color commentary akin to what was broadcast during football games in order to break up the monotony. Finally, after one of those attack and parry combinations, the man twisted his ankle on the churned-up ground and lost his balance. The woman took advantage of the opening with a downward slash and the blade bit into bearded guy's shoulder.

Unfortunately, it continued to travel through, and the next thing anyone knew there was an arm lying on the ground, unattached to the body to which it belonged. The young man cried out in pain as he fell to the ground and tried to plug the bleeding hole with his other hand. The young woman dropped her sword and backed away, looking around for some sort of explanation, horror written across her face. The crowd all began jabbering at once.

Several of the mystics who had disintegrated the body after the first fight rushed out to the injured man. Two held him down and tried to calm his hysterics while a third retrieved the arm and placed it over the wound. Once again they began chanting, and a light, centered on the man's shoulder, enveloped them. After several seconds the light faded and the healers backed away. The injured man gave his arm a few tentative swings and relief flooded over his face as he realized that it moved just as well as it had before. In spite of this relief, he was shaken by the experience. Assisted by his healers, he stood up on wobbling feet, retrieved his sword from the ground, and walked out of the arena, head held high.

"I'm guessing that wasn't according to plan?" Chuck remarked dryly when it became evident that the injured man was going to be ok.

Eddie turned to hush him while his father stomped out into the arena. "Yes," he said. "That wasn't supposed to happen. That blow was certainly going to be a fight-ending hit, but he should only have lost consciousness as his body's energy was siphoned to fuel the healing process. He would have awoken later with some bad memories and a wicked scar." The Warlord's son looked uncertain. "This is bad. Real bad. Not the sort of thing that my father needs right now, particularly given the sentiment against him. His brother wasn't the only one of the opinion that we are headed in the wrong direction."

"Why, is it his fault that this happened?" Allison had

returned at the sound of confusion and had heard Eddie's description.

"No, of course not. But that doesn't mean that people won't take it as a sign. And if it doesn't get solved quickly, he may find himself fending off quite a few more challengers over the next weeks. Assuming he can continue to do so."

The Warlord was in heated discussion with the healers out in the middle of the arena. He was pointing his finger toward one of the sides of the tent emphatically while they shook their heads. Whatever he wanted them to do, they didn't seem willing, and it seemed as if he was starting to reach the end of his patience. Frustrated, he grabbed hold of one of the men by the hair and yanked downward while bringing his own leg up. Knee and forehead met with a loud crack and the healer dropped to the ground. There was sudden silence throughout the entire tent as everyone held their breath.

"Whoa." Eddie whispered. "Our people's mystics are outside the chain of command. Technically, they don't have to do what my father asks them to do, which is why they were refusing him. It is a balance of power sort of thing. This...is unexpected."

There was something of a standoff in the middle of the tent, with the warlord's arm outstretched and pointing again. After several long moments, one of the other men nodded his head and began to walk to the side, quickly trailed by two others. Soon after, they returned, carrying a large chest between them. They placed it on the ground right in front of their unconscious comrade, only sparing him the slightest glance. The warlord made a hurrying motion, and one opened the chest. None of them moved as they looked downward into the container, and a loud murmur began to work its way through the crowd.

“It…is…missing.” One of the healers said, leading to gasps and cries of outrage from the onlookers.

“Yeah. Pretty unexpected.” Eddie repeated.

CHAPTER 12

The warlord, the mystics (including the one he had brained), and his son had all retired to another tent to discuss their discovery. Without really knowing what else to do, the five friends tagged along behind Eddie. No one stopped them, so they assumed they were welcome. The warlord paced back and forth in front of an empty chair, looking at the mystics and shaking his head. He didn't seem able to put together more than a couple words at a time without stopping and having to take a deep breath. Finally, he stopped and threw himself into a chair.

"So, it's gone. How could this have happened?"

"We don't know, my lord," one replied sheepishly, not making eye contact.

"Don't 'my lord' me. I'm not interested in fake humility and I'm on the verge of introducing the rest of your skulls to my knees, one by one." He took another deep breath and then looked straight into the eyes of the eldest of the mystics. "Algondar. How long have we known each other?"

The man opened his mouth to speak but the Warlord cut him off with a raised hand. "Don't treat me like I'm one of your pupils, or worse, like some city lordling that needs to be pandered to. I just killed my brother out there today, and odds are I'm going to have to fend off another challenger in the next several weeks. This isn't helping. Now think. How could this have happened?"

After a brief pause Algondar replied, "In truth, we have no idea. The wards on the chest were unbroken before we opened it ourselves. We don't keep permanent guards around it, and traditionally never have, simply trusting to its being kept out of sight and out of mind. Why would we? Who would take it and what would they do with it?"

"Is there any way that we can track the magic bound into it?" Even before he had finished asking the question the mystics began to shake their heads. The warlord slammed his fist down in frustration. "So, then what are we supposed to do? We are camped next to one of the largest cities in the world. Assuming it is in there somewhere, how are we supposed to find it? Is it even possible to find it?"

"I don't know the answer to that."

Allison cleared her throat, and the older men in the tent seemed to notice her and her friends for the first time. The warlord's eyes narrowed. "Who are these outsiders, Edmund? What are they doing here and why were they invited to the Challenges in the first place?"

His son stammered a few moments trying to explain something that he didn't quite understand himself before Allison spoke up. "We are friends of your son, and visitors to your camp. We came out here looking for information to help us solve a mystery inside the city walls, and after we met, he invited us to join him for the challenges."

"Ahh. And why are you *here*, in my council chambers?"

"Yes, well, we don't really have a good answer to that. However, it's possible we could be of some help to you if you would like it."

The People's leader rolled his eyes dismissively. "How are you going to help us? You're new here. You don't know a thing about us." Several of the younger mystics took advantage of the distraction to sneak out the back of the tent.

"No," she agreed. "We sure don't. But that might actually help more than you think."

The warlord rubbed his face with his hands for several seconds then said, "OK. I guess it can't make things much worse than they are. My days are numbered anyway. What do you think you can do?"

"Well, let's start at the beginning. You are missing the artifact that keeps your people from killing each other whenever they want to settle a challenge, right?" He nodded his head wearily but didn't say anything, so she continued. "First of all, what is the artifact itself? Is it big? Small? Metal? Wood? What?"

Eddie said, "It is a battle standard." At her look of confusion, he added, "You know, a banner you put on top of a pole to carry into battle. It was our first battle standard, if the lore is correct. A sign of our long history and our ability to survive against the odds."

"Ok, so that's a piece of information right there. It is made out of cloth, no doubt, so could easily be rolled up and hidden by whoever took it." They all nodded.

TJ spoke up. "You said the chest was warded, but the wards were unbroken. Do you know if the wards were actually unbroken, or had they been reapplied by whoever opened the chest?" The remaining mystics looked back and forth at each other.

Algondar said, "No, we don't know. As you may have noticed, the arcane arts are not viewed particularly fondly here, and so few of us have any training along those lines. Rather, we are focused on healing and nature magics. It is possible that someone broke the wards and reset them. I, for one, could not tell the difference, and I am the most senior here."

"Well, no offense, but it's not a particularly challenging thing to do if someone has enough talent. Or the money to buy the talent. With your permission?" TJ squinted at the chest and mumbled a few words under his breath. "About what I figured," he concluded. "I could probably have broken and reset the wards myself without too much trouble." The mystics shot him hostile looks and the Warlord reached for the hilt of his sword. TJ added quickly, "Not that I did, mind you. I'm just saying that I could have if I wanted to."

"So, what you're saying is that the protections on our most important relic were basically worthless?"

"Yeah, more or less." TJ did his best not to rub it in.

Algondar sighed. "So, there we have it."

"Out of curiosity," Chuck asked, "When do you think this thing would have been stolen? Depending on when it went missing, we may be able to track it down. That is, of course, assuming the thief took it for the purpose of selling it somewhere on the black market. You have to admit that this would be an attractive item for the discerning collector."

The remaining mystics looked back and forth before one finally concluded. "It could have happened any time since the last Challenge."

"Why is that?"

"We never open the chest. It is another tradition. We have faith in our ancestors' ability to guide and protect us. Opening the chest would be a sign we lack faith. That was the argument we were having right after the accident." The warlord blushed slightly as one of the mystics rubbed the goose egg that had formed on his forehead.

"Well how long ago was it? A week? Two weeks? A month?"

After a few moments of reflection, the Warlord said, "I'd say two months ago or so. Isn't that right?"

Eddie nodded. "Yes, that's exactly right. I remember that one."

"Two months, huh?" TJ mused.

"Yeah," Allison replied, catching his eye. "Two months." She looked back at Algondar. "Is there any limit to the number of times the same person can be saved from death?"

Eddie piped in with the answer, "Don't think so. Some folks don't know when to quit, and challenge over and over, losing every time." He blushed. "It's saved me twice already."

Allison nodded and looked at her best friend. "Are you thinking what I'm thinking?"

TJ grinned. "I think I am."

"Wha—?" Jimmy looked back and forth between the two of them, forehead knotted in confusion.

"First," she began, "in the last two months there have been a series of kidnappings. Not of ordinary people, but of the type of people who should be able to defend themselves. Fighting types, like Stu. But there are no ransom notes. And more importantly, no bodies, which means these people are being kept somewhere. Add to that the theft of a relic that makes it so that people can fight without being permanently hurt. Coincidence?"

"I think not," concluded TJ.

"Someone is running gladiator fights!" Exclaimed Jimmy, finally putting the pieces together. "With gladiators they never have to replace!"

The warlord nodded. "I can see how that would fit." He slumped down into his chair and sighed. "I hate to ask this, but I can hardly see any alternative. Since you are already working on one piece of the puzzle, maybe you could help us out with the other. If you do, my people will be very much in your debt. As will be I, personally." The mystics all nodded agreement.

TJ smiled. "Well, we'll do our best. However, you may not want to expect too much. I wear a dress, after all." None of the tenters so much as cracked a smile.

CHAPTER 13

Later that day they were back at the Unicorn's common room, sitting at the table and talking about what they had learned. A large roast goose sat in the middle of their table, and they took turns carving off bits of meat to eat with more of the freshly baked bread Habib served. When they had first returned to the inn, the conversation at the other tables stopped, and the dirty looks from other patrons reappeared. Chuck took matters into his own hands by putting everyone else's food and drinks on their own tab. After several rounds of ale their fellow guests' morale had improved considerably. The small diamond he had given Habib to cover the costs improved the innkeeper's morale as well.

Coming back into the city was little more challenging than going out. The guards made a show of being extra vigilant in their inspections of any tenters hoping to enter Providence City. Those with travel papers had their documents inspected thoroughly. Those without were hassled.

When the friends arrived at the gate, however, they were treated differently. Between TJ's robes and Allison's shiny breastplate it was clear that the five were not members of the People, and they were waved through without even the briefest glance at their note from the count. The officer on duty squinted at them, as if trying to place their faces, and made a note on a scrap of parchment. They hoped Hallowell wouldn't think they had fled the city and send his goons after them.

"So, we think we've got most of the pieces of the puzzle together, but we're missing the biggest one." TJ was mostly thinking out loud. "Just because we know why the kidnappings are happening and why the battle standard was stolen, we're no closer to finding either, which is what we are supposed to do. For both groups."

"Well, what else do we know, given what we've found?" Allison began slowly. "Why would someone go to the effort of all this? Personal amusement?"

"Maybe," said Chuck, "though, in my experience, personal amusement is usually only a portion of the explanation. Unless this is some sort of revenge, the primary driver is probably money."

"OK, so that's a good start." She nodded. "They're kidnapping fighting types, and they stole an artifact that lets those people fight to the death over and over again. Let's say that they are doing it for money. What else does that tell us?"

"If they are doing it for money, there's got to be someone willing to pay to see the fights," said TJ. "That is, if they are expecting to turn a profit with this, they have to have patrons that will be willing to pay them for the privilege of either spectating or participating. And that means access to a lot of rich people."

"Such as the inner districts of a large city like this one?" Allison was pleased.

"Yeah, I think that would do the trick," put in Chuck.

"How do we know it's in this city though? What makes you think they're still here?" Jimmy was skeptical. "They could be miles away. If they've left town, we'll never find them."

"Foxglove," replied Chuck.

"Foxglove?" That word didn't seem to help Jimmy's skepticism.

"Yeah. Foxglove. That was the poison that they used to knock out Stu. It's a short duration poison, a couple hours of unconsciousness at the longest. That means that they had to be somewhere they considered safe before the poison wore off." He looked thoughtful. "I guess they could tie him up and stick him in a cart somewhere, but you have to remember that if they are targeting seasoned adventures, they run the risk of the person escaping. If they are the type that has to resort to using poisons, that might not be something they can handle. So, they would want to take them somewhere nearby. And the best part is that once they're there, in range of the People's artifact, you can just shoot any escapees in the back with a crossbow or two. They'll still drop, but won't die."

"OK," pushed Stu. "But that's still not good enough. This city is huge. Even if we say they are in the inner districts, we'd still need to search dozens of blocks of buildings. We're going to have to come up with something better. I have no interest in that sort of search and I'm sure that Hallowell isn't going to send his troops marching through the most affluent part of town kicking in doors. I don't care what his relationship to the town's rulers is, that isn't something they are going to stomach. We need to narrow it down even more."

"Well," began Jimmy, speaking slowly so his words didn't outrun his thought process. "Think about what we saw today. A place designed specifically for two people to duke it out to the death. Did you notice how much space they left for the combat? The tent was huge, and the bleachers were only around the perimeter, giving them a really big area in which to fight. Now imagine that you had three or four or even five people all fighting at once. Tenters, who fight with a giant sword like me and the warlord's brother. Or people like Stu, who is okay with a sword if he has to be, but is really an archer. How are you going to accommodate them, *and* leave room for the spectators bankrolling the whole thing?"

"What we're looking for is a building large enough to be used as an arena, and there can't be many of those in the inner districts!" Allison looked triumphant. "Now THAT is what I call a lead." With that, she reached for the full mug of ale in front of her, lifted it in a salute, then took a giant gulp. Her face contorted at the taste of the bitter brew and she said, "OK, so now that I've done that, I'm going back to juice."

The remainder of the evening was spent in light conversation, now that they had some solid ideas to pursue the following morning. When night had fallen and the friends were ready for bed, they returned upstairs. Before they went into their respective rooms, TJ cautioned, "Can you guys please try to stay in tonight? We've already taken plenty of risks, and you know you're never supposed to split the party." He looked at Stu. "I recognize that sleeping under a roof is difficult for you, but you have to remember that I've spent weeks sleeping under trees and in caves and under wagons, and I've managed to survive. You can tough it out for another night or two until we get this thing wrapped up, OK?"

Stu met his stare for a few seconds before finally nodding in agreement. TJ elicited the same promise from Chuck, who was perfectly happy giving his assurance. After all, the rogue knew from the prior night's experience that he wasn't going to learn much of anything from any of the traditional sources. As an outsider no one would talk to him, particularly with armed squads going around kidnapping people. Besides, he had come to the conclusion that he would suffer no ill effects—in truth or within his conscience—for going back on such a promise. It was liberating to finally realize that he didn't need to do what he promised so long as he didn't care how people would react. And in fact, he didn't care one bit.

TJ again set wards in the hallway, this time adding alarm wards on the windows of each of their rooms as well. His were substantially more complicated than the ones that had been used to protect the artifact chest, so he was sure that whoever was behind all this wouldn't be able to break in. He didn't really expect them to try again after the failure to nab Stu, but it took no effort on his part and it was better to be safe than sorry.

Just past midnight Chuck woke up to noises coming from the roof, and he slipped out of bed to open the window to hear better. When he did so, the alarm claxon in TJ's head began blowing and the wizard bolted upright. He grabbed Jimmy from his bed, rushed out into the hallway and banged on Chuck's door. Jimmy, who was alert and battle-ready within moments of being roused, simply kicked at the door, splintering the wooden frame and bending the latch out of alignment. The large man charged into the room, brandishing long knives rather than his great sword on account of the close quarters only to have to duck a dagger aimed at his head. The blade missed him by a hair and embedded itself firmly in the wall.

"What the?" Jimmy and Chuck exclaimed at the same time.

The smaller man had another dagger out and ready to fly but put it down when he realized who had stormed into his room. "What are you doing?" He shouted. "Are you crazy? I could have killed you. Don't you know how to knock?"

"First," Jimmy replied, "Be honest. You haven't got a ghost of a chance of killing me. That aside, what's going on in here? Are you guys okay?" He inspected his surroundings and then peered at TJ, who looked about uncomfortably.

"Are we okay?" Stu grumbled from under the pillow atop his head. "Of course we're OK. I was sound asleep until you woke me up."

TJ sighed. "The alarm ward on your window went off.

I was worried they were coming back for a second try tonight, and didn't want to miss them, or lose one of you guys. What were you doing, anyway? You promised to stay in tonight!"

"I heard noises on the roof and stuck my head out to look. That's it. Honest." Chuck answered immediately.

Allison stuck her head through the door. "What's going on? I miss anything?" Her long hair was a bird's nest of tangles but she gripped her mace tightly.

"No," everyone said at once. TJ added, "Go back to bed. False alarm, everything is okay." Her eyes narrowed, thinking they were trying to trick her, and he added with a wry grin, "Situation normal. We're all fine here now, thank you. How are you?"

"Okeydokes," she replied with a curt nod, and turned around to find Habib standing there tapping his foot, an angry look on his face. A larger version of Grant stood behind the innkeeper, glowering menacingly.

"What are you doing to my inn?" He cried. "This is two nights in a row. It doesn't matter how much you pay me, or on whose business you are on, you can't keep doing this. I have a reputation I need to uphold, and that's not possible with you starting fights and kicking in doors and doing who knows what else every night. No more! The next time something like this happens, you are out the door and that's that. Do you understand?" His eyes flashed in anger and a little blood vein on the side of his head pulsed rapidly.

"My good man," Allison began, attempting to look as imposing as possible, but even with her magical ring on her finger he didn't back down. He stared at her until she bowed her head and said, "Yes, sir. We will be sure there are no more disturbances."

Habib nodded curtly and turned on his heel, heading back downstairs to his own living quarters. His bruiser, on the other hand, remained conspicuously present, arms crossed impassively. As with the night before, there were no appearances by the other guests, though Allison guessed she and her friends would be on the receiving end of the reproachful looks at breakfast again. Not that she blamed them. In her old life, if she'd heard someone kicking in a hotel room door, she would have hidden under the bed and pretended to be invisible too.

"OK, guys. I'm sorry," TJ said when Habib had disappeared. He seemed to be including Grant's brother in his apology. "Over reacted, jumped to conclusions, yeah, yeah. It won't happen again. Hopefully. Anyway, we've still got quite a bit of night left, so let's all get back to sleep and we'll meet up for breakfast, OK?"

Chuck and Jimmy both nodded agreement. Allison began shuffling back to her room and Stu was already snoring.

As predicted, there were a lot of angry looks directed at the friends from the others in the common room the following morning, and at least one angry discussion between a patron and Habib. For his part, the innkeeper was trying to smooth things over, hoping to keep the patronage of both his regular customers and the extremely rich newcomers. It didn't appear to be working. Once the argument ended he approached their table and sat down heavily. He reached out and tore a large piece of bread from the loaf that was sitting on the table.

"Look, friends." He began. "I recognize that you have issues that you are dealing with. I don't know what they are, and I don't want to know what they are. I mean, I'm not unsympathetic. But like I said last night, this can't continue. You've paid me well, and I'm not one to complain, but the money you gave me is going to run out and I'll need to be able to rent rooms to others. I can't have the more affluent clientele looking somewhere else for their lodging and evening entertainment. Mine is one of the nicer inns in this district, and I'd like to keep it that way. There are hostels and other inns that are more suited for… mercenaries and the like." He stopped and looked each one in the eyes in turn. "Do you understand my situation?"

They all nodded, and Allison said, "We understand completely. If you would like, we can pack our things today and find somewhere else to stay for however long we need to remain in Providence City. We would be happy to pay you for your door, and your trouble." She removed her purse from her belt, but Habib enclosed her hands within his own.

He shook his head. "No, my lady. I told you last night that you had one more chance, and I stand by that statement. If something happens again tonight, however, I will indeed take you up on your offer."

"That is fair. In the meanwhile, we will finish our breakfast and be about our business for the day," she replied dismissing him. He nodded and stood.

"Good day to you all. I hope that your business is fortunate." He gave one more bow-bob and turned away.

When he had gone back to the counter to arrange another platter of food Jimmy asked, "So, what's the plan?

Kicking down more doors and stuff?" Allison giggled, but TJ scowled.

"Well here's what I think," The wizard began. "One, we think they are hiding in the inner districts. Two, we think they're running a pit fighting operation. Three, this means they'll need a lot of space for both fighters and spectators." He ticked off the points on his fingers. "That's far more information than we were given to start with. Let's go report back to Lord Hallowell with what we've learned. Maybe that'll be good enough to let us get out of here. Or at the very least maybe he can provide some extra help hunting this place down."

The others at the table nodded their agreement. It wasn't a perfect plan, and it wasn't a sure thing, but it was the best they had going for them. Without any other leads, returning to Hallowell was their only real choice.

CHAPTER 14

"How sure are you about this?" The friends were back in Hallowell's office and had filled him in on all that they had learned, including Stu's attempted kidnapping. The door was once again closed, his assistant Winston standing nearby. The group felt a collective sense of déjà vu standing there uncomfortably while the city's castellan regarded them from behind his desk. They had come by their own choice, so they were less rattled than during their first visit, but it was still uncomfortable meeting with someone who had threated you with death if you decided not to do what he wanted.

"Eh," said TJ half-heartedly. "Not terribly, but we've got nothing else to tell you. We're sure the People are innocent in all this. They've lost a few of their own in the last two months, and the warlord definitely wasn't faking his reaction to the discovery that their precious artifact was missing. So, snooping around out there is a complete dead end. Chuck, who is our, um, information gathering specialist—"

Hallowell cut him off, "And forger."

"…our information gathering specialist," TJ continued, "spent some time poking around inside Providence City itself."

"And there's nothing to be found," concluded Chuck curtly. "Look, let's not blow smoke at each other, OK? You should know that I'm not going be trusted one whit by the Guild. I'm a complete stranger to them, and for all they know I could be an informant working for the government." Hallowell raised his mug, ceding the point. "In fact, at a couple places I visited I was lucky not to have been shanked. No one's talking to me any more than they are talking to your guys. So, what we've got is your best bet. That is, unless there's something you've been holding out on us about. Is there?" After several long seconds of silence, he repeated the question. "Is there?"

Hallowell exchanged a glance with his aide and let out a loud sigh. "All right. I admit it. I haven't been entirely forthcoming with you. Your showing up when you did was an extreme stroke of luck for me, and I wasn't about to let it pass without making the most of it. My men haven't been able to find any information about what has been going on because I was forbidden from looking into it." He rolled his eyes as he continued. "I'm sure you'll be shocked to discover that my position is a political one, and that I am not always allowed to pursue my investigations to their completion." He waved his hand. "This usually happens when some minor lordling drinks too much and gets in a fight in some bar. Maybe he even skewers someone. Is it just? No. Is it life? Yes. I don't make the rules; I just try to enforce them as best I can.

"So, the point to all this is that I needed you to do this investigating for me precisely because I couldn't set my regular men to do it. I told you we were being shut down so you would be subtle in your investigation and wouldn't go spreading my name about. That would have made my position here uncomfortable, to say the least. I couldn't even have my irregulars look into it, because I have no doubts that some, if not all, are reporting to other people of power in the town. The only one I trust completely is Winston, here, which is why both our meetings have been here, with the door closed, and no witnesses." His assistant gave a slight bow. "You, on the other hand, are new to town, with no established relationships. No anything, really. You are the perfect investigators. And the fact that they took a crack at nabbing Stu was even more perfect. It gave you all the more reason to investigate. Everyone understands revenge.

"Of course, your explanation fits into this perfectly. My being shut down on this investigation made no sense. A bunch of random kidnappings was hardly the sort of thing that I would usually be dissuaded from looking into. But let's say there is an underground gladiator arena somewhere in town, catering to the rich and powerful. We certainly aren't squeamish here in Providence City, and a nice fight to the death is a good bit of fun every now and again, but kidnapping people and having them fight to the death over and over again…well that's pretty clearly over the line. No wonder I was told to let it go. If this got out it could get very messy for some pretty important folk."

Allison interrupted him. "So, you believe us? Does that mean you'll let us go?" The hope in her voice was almost too much to stand.

He shook his head with a grim smile. "Unfortunately for you, no, we're not done. Finding that last piece of the puzzle is admirable, and I am grateful for it. But it is insufficient to win your freedom. I still can't get my men directly involved, for the same reason I couldn't have them doing the investigation. Until we know exactly where this is going on and who is running it, it all has to be completely off the record and unofficial. Any connection between me and what you are doing will end up getting the investigation stifled and me most likely sacked." He didn't need to say that their own fate would be far worse.

"What are we supposed to do?" Chuck was frustrated. "You can't really expect us to go door to door, can you? We've got no authority here and can't very well pretend to be the chamber pot inspectors."

"Well, about that, I have an idea." He motioned Winston over and whispered in his ear before sending him from the room. "He is going to take a little while, so how about some refreshments while we wait?" He reached behind him to pull on a rope hanging from the ceiling. The soft sound of bells drifted in from behind one of the walls, and a moment later a servant in the livery of the Watch came in.

"My lord?"

"A jug of wine please, and a tray of fruit and cheese. The sooner the better, please. My guests are hungry and thirsty."

When the servant had left, Stu said, "Actually, we just had breakfast not so long ago."

"Well then, *I* am hungry and thirsty," replied Hallowell. "And the servants tend to be quicker for guests than for the regulars here. It's a hospitality thing, I guess. Or familiarity breed contempt. One or the other." They sat in silence for a few minutes while they waited for the food and wine to come. When it had dropped off by a servant, Hallowell made a motion with his hand and said, "Go ahead and close that door again."

The castellan helped himself to a plate of food from the tray on his desk and poured a large glass of wine, saying, "Please, eat. Never turn down a free meal, especially when you don't know when the next one is coming." He began munching on a wedge of cheese.

Jimmy grunted and began to fill a plate for himself. Having thus broken the ice, the other four all made plates as well, though only Jimmy had any of the wine. He had clearly taken on the constitution of his character and the strong drink had little effect on him. The others, however, were more worried about compromising their clear-headedness. As they munched, Hallowell kept his peace, not interested in volunteering any additional information, until Allison asked, "What exactly did you send Winston off to go do? What are we waiting for?"

"We're waiting for a couple of things," he said between chews. "First, for you to gain access to the inner districts, you are going to need paperwork. You may as well get the real deal, rather than having to rely on your…information gathering specialist." He cast a bland look toward TJ, who let his gaze wander everywhere about the room other than back at the castellan. "Winston is arranging that for you. You'll be able to move freely and without having to carry that pesky note from me that ties your movements to my office. In retrospect, that was a poor decision on my part, but what's done is done." He took a long drink from his goblet.

"The other thing he's doing is collecting some maps. Every several years or so we update the official surveys of each of the districts within the city. You would be amazed at how much a place like this can change in the span of even six months. A building goes up, a building burns down. A road gets choked off by shanties, which then grow to be permanent structures. If we were to wait even as long as five years before revisions the maps would be useless. As it happens, we completed our most recent update earlier this year, so we should have a very good view of exactly how the inner districts are built. Given the parameters that you've come up with, we ought to be able to narrow the possibilities down to just a handful, and at that point it can be a surveillance job. We'll keep an eye on the most likely places and maybe something will show up."

"What do you expect us to see? Someone with a sandwich board over their shoulders saying, "Come see our illegal gladiatorial combat?"" Stu didn't sound hopeful.

"No, but we know from your own personal experience that they are still actively trying to, ahem, recruit additional participants. Perhaps you can catch them coming back in with new recruits. Once we know for certain which building they're housed in, I can muster some troops for a quick raid and catch them red handed. At that point I won't have to worry about obstructions to the investigation.

Anyone who tries to stop me will look like they're part of the conspiracy, whether or not they actually are. No one will want to risk that."

"You mean someone would want to stop you even if they're not involved?" Allison, ever innocent, was surprised.

"Oh sure. Men like me have enemies who want to get in the way of anything I do. Maybe knock me down a peg or two, even get me fired. Others think I'm too much of a busybody and unimportant people being kidnapped are, well, unimportant. It's rather pathetic, actually, how hard it is for me to do my job."

"You've really thought this through, haven't you?" Asked TJ.

"You bet I have. I hate when people get in my business, and this time the pressure was somewhat more forceful than what have to deal with on a regular basis." His face took on a look of hard determination. "So I have indeed been thinking about what I would do once I had the information necessary to make a move. I had hoped to have had this done a couple weeks ago, but was unable to get the break I needed until today. Now I'm itching to get this thing over with."

There was a knock on the door and Winston poked his head in. Hallowell motioned him to enter and when he did the friends saw he was carrying two long, rolled up parchments. He placed them on the table and the castellan unrolled them, one atop the other, securing the corners with wine goblets to keep the papers flat. Each was an extraordinarily detailed map of one of the inner districts. There were street names, of course, but most of the buildings were labeled not only with what they housed—merchants, craftsmen, apartments, but also the tenants for each. In a number of places there were dotted lines connecting one building to another, which Hallowell explained to be "secret" tunnels. Someone had gone to a quite a bit of trouble to make sure that whoever had this map knew exactly where everyone and everything was in the city.

"These are my personal maps. The official ones don't have quite this same level of detail," he chuckled, "but I have found that it is a lot easier for me to do my job if I have a bit more information than everyone else. Not many people know about these, so I would appreciate your not blathering about them. I would, of course, deny their existence, but it would be simpler for all of us if I didn't have to. Now let's take a look and see what we can see."

Everyone but Stu stood over the maps searching for buildings that might be large enough to house the operation they were looking for. Allison looked at where he sat in the chair munching on fruit. He waved and said, "That's just a confusing mess of lines and colors to me. I won't be much help." He popped another grape in his mouth and she turned back to the map.

"How much area do these maps cover?" Chuck pointed to several places on the map. "These here and here look large enough, but I don't know the scale."

"Fifty feet to the inch," replied Winston when Hallowell looked up for the answer. "Maybe not exactly, but within a half a foot or so in most cases."

Chuck shook his head. "Ok, well then that means none of those are going to work. You have to figure that the actual arena space is going to have to be a good hundred feet or so in a square. Otherwise there wouldn't have been any point in trying to nab Stu. And then we have to add in room for spectators and any side rooms. We're going to be looking for a building that's at least this big." He spaced his fingers apart by a little more than two inches and then started moving it around on the map looking for any buildings that might fit the bill.

"There's one, and there's another." He continued to move his fingers about but stopped when it was clear that there were no other buildings the right size. "Two on this map. What are those?"

"Hrm," said Hallowell, squinting at the words written on the buildings. "That one is the temple of Elias. I've been inside there several times, and while the structure might be big enough when looking at it on this map, the inside is crowded with benches for worshipers as well as several altars. Not to mention it is completely public. Not going to have anything like that going on in there."

"What about a basement?" Allison asked.

"Nope. I've been down there myself. There are catacombs where they have buried dead priests and particularly generous patrons over the years. It's a sacred space, and they wouldn't permit any fighting down there. Not to mention the fact that there would be no place for anyone to watch."

"The other one?"

"Well, that one is just a warehouse run by one of the textile cartels in town. I've never been inside that one, though there are wagons coming in and out on a regular basis, loaded down with goods. Not that that really means anything, I guess. It could be the same wagons with the same bundles every time, of course. We can mark it down as a possibility, though I wouldn't have expected that to be the one. None of the pressure I was getting was from anyone connected to the building's owners. In fact, they are generally on the straight and narrow as far as most things go. Let's take a look at the other map and see if we come up with any options there before we jump to conclusions."

He slid the first map out from under the goblets and carefully rolled it again, then handed it to his aide. Almost immediately everyone could see that there weren't any matches in the second district. None of the buildings were at all close to the right size to fit what they were looking for. He rolled that map up as well and put it aside. "Well, I guess we know where to go, though I am still surprised it's that particular group of people. I'm going to need you to do a little more investigating to make sure, so I don't go charging in with my boys and discovering it was all a big mistake. This is still all based on the assumption that you're correct, and it could be that your guess about what this is all about is wrong."

"Well it's not like we can say no, so I guess it's back out into the field we go," grumbled TJ. "When are you going to have those papers done for us?"

"Should be done any time now. The actual document production isn't a difficult process. The trick is in getting all the proper approvals through the government channels. Of course, I AM the government channels, so it's not that hard for me to get it done, especially for a group of fine, upstanding and righteous caravan guards looking for work and who have the very best of references. Again, your references would be me." There was another knock on the door and he said, "I bet those are them, now. Come in!"

A man in dressed in a nondescript tunic entered with some papers in his hand. He gave Hallowell a quick bow, placed them on his table and asked, "Is there anything else I can do for you, my lord?"

"No, that will do, thank you very much for getting this done for me so quickly." The man bowed again and retreated through the door, closing it behind him.

"So here are your documents. This will give you permission to go anywhere in the city without any difficulty." He opened the first map back up and pointed at the warehouse again, then slid his finger slightly. "Right here is a tavern with open air seating. It's that sort of a neighborhood. Expensive shops and the like. Try not to start any fights, because the Watch will come down on you quickly, and if you turn up here again for doing something wrong, it's going to be pretty tough for me to smooth things over. Any questions?"

Chuck raised his hand. "So, all we're supposed to do is determine if this is the place or not? And once we have that information we get back to you?"

"Yes. That is pretty much it. Considering what they most likely have arrayed in there, it's going to take more than just five people to clean them out. If you can confirm that it's going on in the warehouse, we'll call ourselves even and you can go your merry way."

"What about the artifact?" Chimed in Stu. "We should take it back to the People. It would be an excellent sign of goodwill toward them; it seems to be a really important part of their culture. Not to mention, it's exactly what a group of fine, upstanding and righteous people would do."

An irritated look passed over Hallowell's face. "Yes, yes, you can take that with you. That is honestly the least of my concerns." He waved his hand dismissively.

"Works for us. Let's get out of here." The others nodded agreement. Chuck grabbed another handful of grapes before getting up, opening the door, and leaving. Allison blushed slightly and muttered an "excuse us," before following the rest of her friends.

Hallowell smiled, waved and called after them, "Have fun!" Then he poured himself another drink.

CHAPTER 15

"And I would like the duck, please, and a glass of chilled juice." Allison handed the menu back to the waiter with a smile. When he had left, she continued, "I feel kind of guilty eating here instead of with Habib, but I have to say that this is the best part of our job since this whole thing began. I never expected we'd find a real restaurant in this place."

"Don't feel too guilty, Allie. In fact, I'm willing to bet he's happier the less we're around, and I don't blame him," Jimmy said, waving a baguette for emphasis. "I'm pretty sure that we aren't good for his business, even if he said he wanted to give us another chance. I hope this all gets wrapped up today. I want to get a good night's sleep for once, without having to worry about people trying to steal one of us or getting yanked out of bed by an overzealous wizard." He looked at TJ at that last, who shrugged at him.

"Whatever." Said wizard was unimpressed.

The day had a slight chill to it, but there was virtually no wind, so the air was comfortable. Clouds had rolled in during the morning, promising rain later that evening, but for the time being they were enjoying the weather. The tavern in which they ate was directly across the street from the warehouse they had been sent to investigate. It gave them an unobstructed view to the front door, as well as an angle to view into the alley on one side.

Lunch came and the friends enjoyed the best food they had eaten in quite some time. Truth be told, it was better than most of the food they had eaten in the real world as well. None of them came from families where they could spend a couple hundred dollars on lunch for five, which was essentially what they were doing. When they had first sat down, Allison had asked the waiter whether he would accept one of the gems as payment. Just like Habib, the waiter's eyes nearly bulged out of their sockets and he nodded vigorously.

Their time sitting there, however, did nothing to give them any of the information that they were looking for. Whether it was just a slow day or something else, there were no wagon deliveries to the warehouse, nor any wagons leaving, so they were never able to get a look through the door. They saw no one going in or out of the alleyways either, and according to the map in Hallowell's office there were no secret tunnels underneath.

"Well, other than lunch, which I have to admit was quite nice, this has been a total bust," commented TJ. "We can order a dessert, but we can't keep sitting here all day, even if they'll let us buy the spot. We stick out like sore thumbs, compared to the rest of the clientele here." He was right. All the other patrons and most of the passersby were dressed in upper class fashion. Jimmy, with his bulk and enormous sword, simply didn't fit in, and virtually everyone's heads turned in their direction as they walked past.

"Well, there's always tonight," Chuck suggested. "I can come and set up a watch overnight to see if anything fishy goes on."

"That would work if we thought they were out kidnapping every night," said Stu. "If people were disappearing every night Hallowell would have said so. Not to mention it would be a lot harder to shut down his investigation with that sort of crime spree."

"OK, then how about I come for a visit overnight and take a peek inside. It's a warehouse." He waved a hand dismissively. "I've been in and out of hundreds just like it over the years." By now no one even batted an eye at the suggestion that he'd had years of experience, despite their only being in the world for a few weeks. "I can pop in, snoop around, and be back before you know it."

"How many of those hundreds of warehouses you've been in were potentially armed camps filled with gladiators who couldn't die?" Allison countered.

"Not too many, I must admit." Chuck said. At her raised eyebrow he added, "OK. None. So, it would be a bit more…difficult. Aren't our teachers always telling us to challenge ourselves?"

"Not ones that would get you killed," she countered.

"Yeah, well there is that. Still, how many times have we

all almost gotten killed and made it out alive? We're the heroes!"

"Simon was one of the heroes too."

The mood at the table suddenly dropped by a couple notches at her comment and no one said anything for several long minutes. The waiter came and hovered around the table, but when he was completely ignored he went back inside.

"Hey, I have an idea," Allison exclaimed. Without explaining further, she stood up from the table and took a last swig from her glass of juice. She then marched straight across the street and banged on the warehouse door with her fist while her friends looked on in horror. After several moments she banged on it again, louder.

"What are you doing?" hissed TJ from where he still sat, though there wasn't really much point in keeping quiet.

She waved him off and then banged a third time. The sound of a latch being drawn came from inside the warehouse and then the door opened inward a small amount, revealing a short man in a robe. Seeing the door open, the others scrambled up and ran to assist Allison in case she needed some help. "May I help you?" The man asked.

"Greetings, friend. My name is Allison. Um, Allison Treeweave. I represent a number of my colleagues who are freelance protection specialists. We are recently arrived to Providence City, but as you can see," she held out her newly issued travel papers, "we have been vouched for and have been granted full access to all the districts here. We are looking for work, and we heard that you typically do a brisk business in textiles out of this facility. We would like to provide you full service protection if you are so inclined. As it happens, we even have a specialist in urban environments with us who would prove invaluable should you care to employ us." She gave a bow.

The man looked completely surprised by her offer and stood staring at her for a few moments before saying, "Well we typically hire from the mercenaries' guild rather than dealing directly with unknown and unbonded individuals." He looked them up and down with a calculating eye before saying, "Please wait here one moment," and closing the door. The bolt clicked back in place and TJ hissed at Allison again.

"What are you DOING? We are supposed to look around, not ask to be hired. Now if we had any chance of sneaking in, that's totally blown."

She shrugged back at him and said, "Well we'd already decided the stakeout was a bust, so we may as well see if we can't salvage something."

Just then the latch sounded again and the door opened, this time wider. "Please come in for a moment." The friends looked at each other, and walked in hesitantly.

"This is our caravan master, Alquin Therris, and he may decide whether or not you will be of any value to us." The man gave a little bow and retreated to a side room.

It took only moments for all five to realize that this was not the place they were looking for. The warehouse was vast, and was full, top to bottom with bolts of cloth. There were tables with cutting implements, racks and shelves bolted to the floor, and ladders on wheels for reaching the upper levels. There was no conceivable way someone could convert this into an arena.

After twenty minutes with the caravan master, who promised to consider them for future service, they returned to the restaurant to settle their bill. Dejectedly, they began the trip back to the Dancing Unicorn, their only real lead a dead end.

CHAPTER 16

Habib's smile faltered only a little as the five friends trudged back through his common room and up the stairs, only Allison sparing him the barest of smiles in response to his boisterous welcome back to the inn. "I hope to see you for supper later this evening," he called up to their retreating backs before returning to the demands of his other patrons.

The other three followed Chuck and Stu into their room, and Allison closed and bolted the door behind them. Chuck and TJ sat together on one bed and Stu and Allison the other. The room's only chair was constructed of delicate-looking wicker and was far too small for Jimmy's bulk, so he plopped down on the floor and leaned his back against the door. For several long moments no one spoke, the mood among them dark and heavy. At last Stu answered the unspoken question, "Well, we've done our best. I don't know about any of you, but I'm ready to get out of here. This city is quickly sucking the life out of me, and I'd rather brave a wall guard's crossbow than waste away here among the brick and mortar." He made an exaggerated show of sniffing in the air before adding, "And the smells."

TJ looked thoughtful. "I'm inclined to agree. Those gate guards didn't appear especially vigilant when we passed through. And now that we're back in our rooms I can bring my spellbooks along. We've got plenty of money, and there's nothing tying us to this place. In fact, we could even go to the Mysterium, where I completed my magical studies. If one of my old masters doesn't have the ability to send us home, perhaps we could find what we need in its library. There's no more extensive collection on the continent, or perhaps even the planet." "Except for that whole quest thing," replied Jimmy. "You've heard what people have been saying just the same as I. This city's allying, or not allying, with the Arcanum could make all the difference between his success in the west. If we bug out now and they throw in with him, we may be stuck here forever." He slammed his fist down on the chair for emphasis, and was dismayed to discover it went straight through a crosspiece, sending splinters flying in every direction. After a moment of stunned silence he continued, "I don't want to be stuck here. I like being Jimmy the kid from Massachusetts, not Jameson the northern barbarian who crushes furniture when he gets frustrated. I think we were brought here specifically to defeat that crazy wizard and we aren't getting back home until we do."

"Well you're assuming two things," shot back TJ. He

held up a finger. "First, that what we do here will make any difference whatsoever as to whether Providence City signs an alliance. There's no guarantee that even if we solve this mystery anyone is going to care what we think. The city's leaders have to make their decisions on behalf of all those thousands of others who live here, not just what we want them to do. Or," he added with a wry smile, "at least on behalf of their own self-interests, not just what we want them to do. Second," he held up another finger, "we've been working on the assumption that we want Magnus to fail his conquest. If anyone's going to have the power to send us back, wouldn't it be him? Maybe we should be helping him, not fighting against him."

"So that he can enlist others like Crackrock to act as enforcers, TJ?" Asked Allison. "Don't you remember what Thaddeus said?"

"You mean the murderer, Allie? The one who got us all into this mess in the first place?" TJ smirked and even Jimmy snorted.

"Well yeah, him." Allison looked momentarily uncertain. "But he seemed pretty honest about what he thought would happen, that's for sure. Not all wizards are good people like you and those you learned from, you know. I saw some of that years ago at the Temple. Jimmy can back me up on that."

The barbarian nodded his head vigorously as memories came unbidden into his head. "Yeah, some of the stuff I've seen, TJ." He shook his head turned to spit, only at the last moment catching himself and avoiding making a mess on the floor.

"Yeah well I'm still not convinced," TJ frumped.

"What about you, Chuckles?" Jimmy called over to the rogue, who had leaned backwards and now lay with an arm draped over his eyes. "You've been strangely silent through all this."

The smaller man heaved a deep breath and sat back up. "Me? I don't even have an opinion." He paused a second as if trying to organize his thoughts. "No, that's not true. I've got an opinion, and it's a pretty strong one. But I don't think it's *my* opinion, if you get what I mean. Since the other night out on the rooftops, I've been feeling my old life pulling on me more and more. My first instinct is to ditch all of you. Before I teamed up with you folks, I'd only really ever had one partner in my life, and, well, suffice to say that didn't end so well, for either of us. I could be out that window and gone in thirty seconds and you'd never see me again no matter how hard you looked.

"I'm pretty sure that's not the right choice, but I'm not at all sure what is, so I'm going to keep my mouth shut. What I will say, however, is that if you folks want to go, I can get you out. I mean *us* out. The gates are pretty tight, even overnight," he snickered at his little rhyme, "but I saw a half dozen places my first night alone where it would be a quick, easy, up and out and we're gone. We could probably buy some horses from Eddie's folks, or I could steal some for you if you'd rather, and we'd be leagues away before anyone even knew we were gone. Just say the word." He leaned flat again, and resumed his arm-over-eyes pose, to all appearances asleep.

The other four looked at his prone form in silent

surprise at how calmly he laid out their options. Their time in the city had clearly returned Chuck to his character's amoral roots as a lock-pick, thief, and who knew what else. He hadn't even batted an eye at the idea of stealing someone's horses. They each wondered to what other lengths he might go on behalf of their quest, or even himself.

"So what's it going to be?" TJ asked, matter-of-factly. "I say we make a break for it. Let these folks solve their own problems. We've got our own issues to look after."

"I'm not proud," answered Stu, "but I agree. I feel a little twinge at bailing out on Eddie and his people, but we never promised them anything. If we had another lead, maybe I'd consider staying another day or two, but if we go back to Hallowell with nothing other than, 'well, we tried,' we're just as likely to end up back in the clink." His face took on a feral look. "I'm *not* going back into that cell, no matter what."

Jimmy looked back and forth between the three and slowly nodded. "I don't want to go back to prison either. And like TJ said, there's no guarantee that anything we do here will make the city elders change their course. We may find it easier to stop the wizard by moving further east. I vote we go."

Three faces looked to Allison, and she met each of their eyes in turn. "Well I don't know why you're looking at me," she said curtly. "You three already outvote me, so I guess the decision is made."

"Oh, don't be that way, Allie," TJ offered, patting her on the knee. "We're a team, after all."

After several seconds, she finally nodded. "I guess you're right. We have no other leads, so the investigation is pretty well dead. I really don't think any of you would run if we had another option, so I guess tonight we make a run for it." The other three nodded their agreement, the matter settled.

Then, in the silence, Chuck asked, "So am I buying or stealing those horses?

CHAPTER 17

Night had fallen and the sounds of the city had almost entirely faded. From time to time the yells of drunken revelers echoed along the streets, but they were few and from far away. The nightly Watch patrols had ceased hours before. Providence City was well and truly asleep.

"I feel like a teenager sneaking out of her room," Allison remarked as she checked the knot connecting a thick hemp rope to the bed frame one last time. The other end dangled out the window and down the side of the inn. "This is ridiculous."

"That's because you *are* a teenager sneaking out of her room," replied TJ over his shoulder. He was bent over his pack, making sure that his spellbook and other arcane necessities were safely stowed. "And if Habib is on Hallowell's payroll, the last thing we want to do is traipse through the front door."

She stuck her tongue out at his turned back. "Yeah,

well, it doesn't make me feel any less ridiculous." She looked to the others. "Are we ready to go?"

"I've been ready since we got here," replied Stu quietly, and Chuck nodded his agreement.

Only Jimmy looked uncertain about the plan, though not because he didn't think they should leave. He was more concerned about the rope and bed frame holding up under his bulk. "Ready as I'll ever be," he finally nodded.

Chuck patted him on the shoulder as he passed by. "Don't worry big guy. With as many hit points as you've got, even if you jumped from the roof you'd still be in plenty good shape. That's what we love about you." The small man peeked one last time out the window before deftly climbing onto the sill and scurrying down the rope. Allison looked over the sill but saw no trace of her friend in the shadows. Several seconds later the silence was broken by a low whistle, the signal that the street was clear for the rest to descend. Stu was second, to provide a second set of trained eyes and an extra sword if necessary. Allison was next, followed by TJ, both darting across the street to the safety of a darkened alley upon reaching the bottom. Cautiously, Jimmy backed out the window, fingers digging into the window sill and legs dangling beneath him. After a single glance below, he transferred first one hand then the other to the rope, and slowly lowered himself down. Almost immediately there was a soft *thunk* and the rope, along with Jimmy, dropped straight to the ground. The large man's limbs flailed wildly as he fell, though as he hit the ground he tucked and rolled, somehow turning what could have broken someone's legs into only scrapes and bruises.

After a quick look left and right, Allison ran to her friend. "Are you hurt?" She asked, looking him up and down for any sign of injury. Jimmy circled one of his arms, grimacing lightly as his shoulder moved, but shook his head.

"Nah, I'm good." He eyed the rope coiled at his feet warily. "Kinda like to know how that happened, though." He picked the cord up, running his fingers over where it had broken. Allison reached out as well, feeling the clean break. As one, the pair turned their eyes up to the window, where the slightest glint of metal embedded in the sill was visible. From behind them came a slight tittering laugh.

"Told ya, Jimmy." Chuck, crouched almost invisibly in a nearby doorway, wore an ear-to-ear grin. "Plenty of hit points." Stu, just up the street, chuffed a short laugh.

Jimmy's face contorted in an angry grimace, and his hand reached for the sword at his back. Allison intercepted his arm and she murmured, "Easy there. Remember, he's your friend." After looking back and forth between her and the rogue several times, he released the breath he didn't know he was holding and nodded his head. His scowl cleared and turned into a smile, revealing the teenage boy within once again.

"Nice one, Chuckles."

"Yeah, nice one," hissed TJ. "Maybe you and Stu could disappear at a moment's notice, but the other three of us are back in the clink if Hallowell learns about this. Quit being a jackass."

Chuck shrugged the insult off. "Dude, it was just a prank. Relax. I wouldn't have done it if the coast weren't clear." Even so, his face turned serious. "Follow me. The wall isn't far." Without waiting for a response, he turned and slipped down the street, darting from shadow to shadow so deftly that even his friends, following close behind, had trouble keeping their eyes focused on him. Stu took up the role of rear guard, and Allison couldn't help but notice he had an arrow nocked in his bow. The ranger's movements reminded her of a tiger she had once seen in a zoo enclosure that was far too small for it. It looked perpetually ready to spring into terrible action the moment it found its way out, and she'd thought at the time about how exhausting it must have been to be always ready to jump into action but never actually be able to.

Chuck's assessment of "isn't far" turned out to be an understatement, as twenty minutes after leaving the inn they were still walking. Whether by Chuck's planning or just happy accident, the group didn't encounter a single soul as they moved. Their initial anxiety had melted into a more relaxed caution, so when a wave of large green bodies came pouring out of one of the alleys they were completely surprised. The wave swept over the friends, bowling Allison over and knocking TJ roughly against a shop wall, then poured silently down the street as a single mass of bodies.

CHAPTER 18

When Allison recovered from the onslaught of green bodies, she found her friends with their weapons out and ready. Chuck was sitting on one of the large green creatures with a dagger pressed against its neck, and Stu stood nearby, a knocked arrow pointed at their captive. The creature lay paralyzed in fear, eyes wide. With the disappearance of the wave of creatures, an eerie stillness returned to the street. If any nearby residents had heard anything, they kept that knowledge to themselves.

"Pleasssse, don't hurt me! Pleasssse." The lizard man—for that was what it was—beneath Chuck spoke with such a blatantly stereotypical snake lisp that Allison actually burst out laughing at the sound. The creature's eyes flashed back and forth between her and Chuck, not understanding the joke and worried that he had been captured by lunatics. "I am not dangeroussss. I promisssse. I jusssst want to go with the resssst of my family. Look. I have no weaponsssss."

"Check him," said Chuck, maintaining his dagger's pressure and keeping his eyes on the creature's face.

Stu stepped closer and gave the lizard man a look over. "Nope, all clear. He's not even wearing clothes, so I don't have to bother frisking him. You can let him up, though I guess there's nothing to keep him from running again."

"Oh yes there is," Chuck replied, twirling the dagger between his fingers as he lifted it from the lizard man's neck. The creature's eyes followed the blade's movement anxiously, then looked back at Chuck's face and gave a nod in understanding. Chuck sheathed the dagger and climbed off its chest, whereupon his captive wiggled its fingers and flexed its arms to test if anything were broken, then sat up.

"Thank you, friendssss. Pleasssse, may I go join my family?" He asked submissively, eyes downcast. "They will be worried about me." He sat up and began to get to his feet.

"Not yet, I don't think," said TJ authoritatively. He too had regained his feet and looked imposing in his wizard robe and hat. "First, you are going to tell us who you are and what you were doing here. We've never seen anyone like you, so I don't think you're a local."

"Pleasssse, friendssss." The lizard man rubbed its hands in an anxious manner. "My name issss Ik'tha'bor, and my family and I live under the ccccity. Or at leasssst we did. We are not bad. We eat fish and ratssss and never come up to the sssssurface. We don't like the ssssun."

"Is that so? And just how long have you been living down there?"

"My father'ssss father'ssss father lived in the sssssewers. Before that no one remembersssss."

Allison, feeling compassion for the scared creature asked in a gentler voice, "Well why did you all leave now then? And in such a hurry."

"There are intruderssss in our home. They come with magicssss and sssswords and they cannot be killed. We shot them with arrowssss but they did not bleed. Sssso we fled. Maybe we will find another home, but firsssst we are going to go to the," he paused a moment in thought, then finished, "sssomewhere elsssse."

The friends exchanged glances with each other. "The sewers," exclaimed Chuck. "Of course!"

Allison asked, "Just how far from here was your home?"

"Not far. Down through the ssssewer drain in the alley way, then walk fifteen minutessss to the ssssouth. We live in a big chamber. You cannot missss it."

TJ made a decision. "OK. Go. You seem harmlessss, er harmless, enough, and your family will no doubt be worried about you. Hurry to wherever you were going, and good luck to you." He looked up and down the deserted street. "You're lucky it was us who you bumped into, and not the Watch. I imagine it would have gone much worse for you."

Ik'tha'bor didn't need to be told twice, and bolted off after the other lizard men, casting anxious glances behind him, as if afraid he was going to be shot in the back. The five stood in awkward silence as they watched him run.

"So…" Allison began, then stopped as she tried to make eye contact with each of her friends. None but Jimmy met her gaze

"So…?" Countered Stu idly, looking off into the distance

She gave an exasperated huff, then blurted, "Oh don't pretend like you don't know what I'm talking about. You all convinced me to leave because we had run out of ideas and didn't know what to do next. Well, we just got a new idea and I'll tell you exactly what we should do. We should go back to Hallowell and tell him what we found."

"Why?" Asked TJ. "He's treated us like crap. We don't owe him anything."

"No, but what about all the people they've kidnapped?' She turned her gaze to Stu. "And what about our new friends outside the walls? We told them we'd try to help. You want to just desert them?" She took a deep breath. "Look, I'm not saying we need to do anything other than report back. Once Hallowell knows what's going on, he can send in his bruisers and sort stuff out himself. But right now we're the only ones who know."

"We could send him a note," offered Jimmy.

"And what if he doesn't get it? What if we give the note to someone part of this whole scheme? Or to someone who just takes our money and tosses the note in the trash? This is too important not to deliver in person."

The four boys looked at each other silently. After several long seconds Jimmy chuckled. "And that's what happens when a temple-trained priestess is your party healer, I guess. She's pretty convincing, isn't she?" He extended his hand to Allison. "I'll see this through."

She took his hand and shook it silently. After a moment TJ nodded, "You're my best friend, Allie. I'm in."

Chuck shrugged. "I still don't even have an opinion. I'll stick it out."

Sighing, Stu removed the arrow from his bow and thrust it back into his quiver. "Well I guess if we're not sneaking out, I'm probably not going to have to shoot anyone." He turned on his heel and strode off in the direction of Hallowell's office, leaving the others to rush to catch up.

The party traveled each in their own thoughts back to the Watch's headquarters, but upon arriving found the building in disarray. Fully armed and armored guards ran back and forth, as did clerks and other servants. Allison pulled one aside and asked what was going on.

"Lord Hallowell has been kidnapped, not thirty minutes ago," he said between gasps for air. "He was in a meeting with some stewards from the government when a group of armed individuals barged in, subdued the lot of them, and carried off both the Castellan and his assistant. No one has any idea how they got in or how they got back out, and everything is in chaos." The man looked around anxiously and said, "I must go report to my superiors. I'm sorry, but really I must go," and took off at a run.

"Report!" snorted Chuck. "He didn't have to report to anyone. I bet he just didn't want to stick around in case we decided to nab him too. Anyway, this doesn't bode well." The others nodded and the group continued to make their way toward Hallowell's office. Several times they were stopped and asked what they were doing, but each time the combination of the newly issued travel papers and the note they had received from the Castellan telling guard gates to let them pass seemed sufficient to let them through. When they finally arrived at his office, Alfred, the officer who had escorted them from their cell, met them at the door, an irritated look on his face.

"Ahh, his Lordship himself told me that you may come here, and I was told to give this to you." Alfred handed Allison an envelope identical to the one they had received the day before, including Hallowell's seal in wax. As soon as she took it, he added, "And now I can get back to my real job, discovering what happened and getting his Lordship back." He gave a curt nod and strode purposefully off.

"Well that was weird," remarked Allison, sliding her finger under the fold and breaking the seal. Her eyes scanned the paper quickly, and then she read it out loud.

Hello, friends

The fact that you are reading this means that something unpleasant has happened to me, and this note's bearer is as honest as I thought he was. I may or may not be alive at this point, though for the sake of argument, let us assume for a moment that I am. As I write this, I have only just sent you away on your task, and so what day you are reading this, I cannot predict. However, one thing I know for certain is that when I set you to work I knew I was stirring up a hornets' nest. The pressures brought to bear on me have been substantial, but I have never bowed to any man's pressure.

What does this mean for you? It means a number of things. First and foremost, it means that your duty to me has been relieved. In truth, you never really had a duty to me at all. I must confess that your detention for aiding criminals was a bit of a fabrication. The man you know as Thaddeus is, in truth, one of my own agents, and while your caravan waited in line he sent someone ahead with a message to me about your qualities. You were precisely what I needed at that moment in time—competent outsiders who could perform an investigation without appearing to work for me.

Second, it means you now have a choice. You may leave Providence City or you may stay and finish what you've started. In fact, those are your only two choices. The fact that I am no longer here indicates that you caught someone's attention with your investigation. You may well be next on their list, so if you do not find a solution to this situation yourself, it will not be safe to stay. If you choose to leave, leave at once.

I have learned through other channels that you are pursuing your own agenda. If I don't see you again, I wish you the best of luck in seeing it to completion. Yours is a noble goal; perhaps the most noble of these dark days, and one I share. As self-serving as this may appear, your choice to stay or leave Providence City bears directly on your quest. Those who have thwarted my investigations and captured or killed me are almost certainly those same ones who would ally with the Arcanum. Should they not be stopped, such an alliance is a virtual certainty.

Please know that you owe me nothing. On the contrary, I have used you poorly, though for what I believe was the right reasons. Whichever path you take, be assured that I hold you in the highest regard, not the least of which for putting your own safety at risk to save my servant's caravan with no expectation of reward.

Should we meet again, I remain

Yours,

Lord Cassius Hallowell

Castellan, Providence City

P.S. Please let your "information acquisition specialist" know that the only reason I knew the documents were forgeries was because my agent knew you produced them. I have never seen more competent work done, even by my own men.

"Huh," remarked Chuck whose face then broke into a grin as he punched Allison's shoulder. "I told you they were good!"

"Huh, indeed," repeated TJ. "Well, this is interesting. We can pack up and get out of Dodge if we want, and get back to doing what we were doing before we got here. We don't even have to sneak out as we go!"

"Whatever it was that we were doing," Chuck said with a dry laugh. "It's not like we really had a plan beyond simply going east, and that was never a particularly good plan in the first place."

"Do you have a better idea?" TJ snapped back.

"Yeah, well maybe I do!" Chuck paused. "Or at least maybe I will, once I think of one."

"Quiet, children," shouted Allison and both heads snapped toward her. When she had their attention she said, "Regardless of what we were doing or not doing, we're here now, and so we have to decide what to do next. I doubt he's lying to us this time. The one thing we can't do is stay put and do nothing. Chances are we know too much about what's been going on, so we are the next obvious targets. Whoever is behind this, they might not be content with a simple kidnaping any more. They may just decide to silence us permanently."

She had everyone's attention now. "What do you propose?" Jimmy asked quietly, cutting off TJ's retort and giving her a subtle wink unseen by the other boys.

"Well what do we know? We've a pretty good idea as to what is going on and where. We offered to help the People get their artifact back, and almost without a doubt it's down in those sewers. There has been a string of kidnappings that we have the ability to solve, not to mention what happened to Stu, which I'm still pretty irked about." She paused a moment. "And not just at Stu. Lastly, and perhaps most importantly if none of those prior reasons are worth anything, you can't deny that if we manage to retrieve the artifact *and* save Hallowell, we will have two extremely powerful men on our side. Men who control thousands of soldiers. Men who would be willing to stand up to the Arcanum magus when he marches west, or even march with us as we go east."

As she had expected, it was the last argument that caught everyone's attention. The tent people disdained magic, so enlisting their aid against a mad wizard bent on world domination seemed like a no brainer, especially if they owed the friends a favor. Securing the Castellan's return was even more important. Thaddeus had claimed that many in the city government were leaning towards siding with the mad wizard, and Hallowell's note confirmed it. If some of those officials were involved in Hallowell's kidnapping, then a major power shift could be brewing in the Providence City government. They all took a few moments to imagine what it would mean to have thousands of soldiers at their back, instead of facing things alone.

At last, TJ declared, "OK, you sold me on it." The other boys nodded agreement. "Let's see if we can't find a quiet room around here somewhere. I'm want to look through my spell book briefly, and I'm willing to bet the rest of you are going to want to check back over your gear before we go charging in after all." He smirked at Allison. After several minutes of poking around they came across am empty reception room where they could prepare themselves for the upcoming fight. They didn't even notice the suspicious glares from guards and servants alike as they checked and rechecked equipment. They had work to do.

CHAPTER 19

Morning light had not even begun to show its face, and downpour had sprung up by the time the five were ready to leave the Watch's headquarters, blotting out even the wan moonlight. Before they left, Stu wrote out a note to Edmund and his father informing them of the plan and bullied a servant into delivering it to the tent city. The young man didn't even question his authority, more than happy to get away from the chaos that still reigned within the building. If all went well the friends would bring the tenters the good news (and the artifact) personally, but if things went poorly, they wanted someone else to know what had happened.

The group returned to the inner districts, where the newly deployed guards were considerably more diligent about checking papers than earlier in the day. Patrols of the Watch had increased substantially, as well, and on the walk they passed several checkpoints that had been set up at busy intersections. Between the kidnappings, and the attack on the count, there was an anxious mood among the guards. Everyone was on edge.

They were about a block away from their destination when they heard a whisper from within an alleyway. "Psssst." The group stopped and drew their weapons, on guard for whoever it might be.

"Who is there?" Jimmy called out quietly.

"It issss me, Ik'tha'bor," the voice replied. "Don't hurt me, pleasssse." The figure of the lizard man Chuck had sat upon resolved in the darkness, hands outstretched in a sign of peace.

"What are you doing here?" Allison asked, putting a hand on Jimmy's arm and giving it a tug. The big man took a step backwards and sheathed his sword. The others similarly put down their weapons. "Weren't you going with your family to wherever it was they were headed?"

"Yessss, I did." He nodded. "My family all made it to the meeting sssspot, and they are waiting there for me. But I came back to sssssearch for you."

"Why?"

"Becausssse I believe that you can help ussss. The ssssewer issss our home. It issss all we know. We do not want to leave. Sssso I came to find you to assssk you for help. Help ussss get our home back."

"What's in it for us?" Chuck spoke just loudly enough to be heard. Allison turned and elbowed him in the ribs.

"We are going there anyway," she said, "so you don't have to give us anything. Isn't that right, guys?" She turned back to Chuck and stared him down.

"Yeah, yeah. Old habits die hard, you know," he grumbled.

"You will do thissss for ussss? Thank you, oh thank you, oh thank you sssso much!" The lizard man got down on his knees and hugged Allison's feet.

"Well don't thank us yet," remarked Jimmy. "We still have to find the place and get rid of them. You wouldn't mind coming to show us the way, would you?"

Ik'tha'bor looked anxious at the thought and rubbed his hands again in agitation. "No, I do not know how to fight, and would jusssst get in your way." He looked thoughtful for a moment. "But there issss ssssomething that I could do. I am very quiet. I can ssssneak down and look around and leave a trail for you to follow. And then you can go down and make them go away from my home. Will that help?" He gave them the lizard equivalent of puppy-dog eyes, as if he really wanted to make them happy and hoped what he was doing was enough.

"Yes, that should do fine. Thank you," said Allison with a smile, and continued, "Lead the way!"

"And if we fail, they can always move to Gary, Indiana," jibbed Jimmy, which made Allison snort a laugh and the poor lizard man look confused.

"Wait here," Ik'tha'bor said, suddenly sounding authoritative. "I will mark the path with an 'X' for you so you know where to go, and when I emerge, I will make a light for you." He then dashed across the street, down half a block and into the alleyway he had emerged from earlier that day.

"Wow, I'm glad he was here," deadpanned Stu. "I would never have known to go down *that* alley."

Allison shushed him. "So now, we wait. And hope he doesn't get caught."

Despite the early hour, the street had become active, as those whose businesses opened with the sunrise made their way to work. Those who walked past gave the friends a wide berth, some going so far as to cross to the other side of the street. Many shot nervous glances over their shoulders, and Chuck said, "I don't like how those people are looking at us. If one of them reports an armed group loitering about to the Watch, this could get ugly for us, especially if whomever they get in touch with is part of this whole conspiracy. Hallowell himself said he didn't trust all of his underlings. We should get out of sight."

Conveniently enough, there was a small temple fronted by a public garden bordered by a low hedge just across from the alley Ik'tha'bor had entered. Although the hedge itself was evergreen and still full, the garden's trees had already lost their leaves and provided no protection from the rain. The five squatted behind the bushes, just out of sight of the street.

Twenty minutes later, a light flashed across the street from them, signaling that Ik'tha'bor had done his job and was leaving. Quietly, Chuck said, "That's our sign," and the five crossed the street and into the alleyway. It was piled high with empty crates and junk that had been tossed to the side. There was a half an inch of standing water on the cobbles and it smelled as if a whole family of somethings had crawled in there to die. A narrow path led through the detritus.

They picked their way through the mess as quietly as

possible, despite the fact that they knew it was unlikely anyone below ground could hear them. At the very back of the alley they discovered a propped-open sewer entrance. Stairs leading downward were barely visible in the morning's dim light. The five looked at each other in silence. "Well, I guess I'm the one to go first," Chuck said, and slowly crept down the stairs, his ears straining for any sign of an ambush. The others gave him a few seconds before following, but soon they were all standing ankle-deep in muck.

"Eww," murmured Allison. "I guess it makes sense since this is a sewer, after all, but still. Eww."

Stu unslung his pack and withdrew a small oil lantern. It was a bullseye lantern, only shining in one direction, with a door that could completely block its light. He deftly struck a spark and lit the lantern's wick. A ray of light sprang forth, illuminating the nearby wall. He then handed the light to TJ and unslung his bow from his shoulder.

The sewer looked much older than the buildings above ground, suggesting that the current incarnation of Providence City was not the original one. The ceiling rose eight feet overhead in an arch, and there was a narrow walkway on either side of a deeper channel down the middle. There must have been a blockage somewhere, since the sewage had spilled up over the lip of the walkway, and the friends' feet sloshed as they walked. There was no way to judge just how deep the central channel was, but they all knew that falling in would be a pretty horrible experience and stayed close to the wall.

TJ searched the walls with the beam of light before stopping at a X and an arrow pointing to their right drawn roughly with chalk. "Guess that's the mark, huh?" He whispered. They set off in the indicated direction, their feet making slight sucking sounds in the muck. The sewers branched off in several places, but at each intersection there was the same X and arrow on the wall telling them the way to go. Stu silently retracted his snide remark about the lizard man's help. Without his assistance they would have quickly been lost amongst the twists and turns.

After a half hour of careful travel, the glimmer of torchlight came into view from around a bend and TJ shuttered the lantern. Chuck raised his hand to stop his friends, then crept forward on catlike feet. Even with the softly glowing light from the torches in front of him, his friends quickly lost track of his movements as he hugged the wall with almost supernatural skill. The others waited in silence, each anxiously straining to hear a shouted alert or the clash of weapons. After only a couple minutes he returned and whispered, "This looks like part of where the Lizards used to live. It's not big enough for an arena, but there are some men in bunks down here, nonetheless. Guards, probably. We are going to have to get past these folks." To TJ he added, "You can open the lantern back up. They aren't being too vigilant. The wizard nodded and light again filled the area.

"How many?" Jimmy had unslung his sword and his eyes began to shine with the prospect of charging into battle. The knuckles on the hand holding his weapon had gone white from the strength of his grip.

"I counted eight, though five are sleeping. I thought about taking the three out myself, but I wouldn't be able to get the last before he noticed the other two dropping, and he would've raised the alarm. Our best bet is to take out the ones standing as quickly as possible and keep the ones in their beds from getting their weapons."

"I can take two standing," said Stu. "If you get the third, the others can rush in and subdue the ones in their bunks."

"Good plan. I'm definitely good for one. Let's go."

Before they set off down the sewer tunnel Chuck bent his knees a few times before springing across the center channel and landing on the other walkway. Allison's jaw dropped open at the feat, as the sewer was easily eight feet wide. He gave her a wink and a smile and turned toward the torchlight. In each of his hands was a throwing knife, perfectly balanced and razor sharp. He and Stu started forward, with the others walking behind the archer.

Rounding the bend, they found themselves in a gallery that was at the meeting point of five different tunnels. The sludge in four of them were flowing slowly into the central pool, with the fifth, larger tunnel, carrying it away. As Chuck had said, there were three men standing guard with weapons ready. One looked down the larger tunnel and the others each looked back and forth between two of the smaller ones. It was one of these smaller tunnels that they had been walking down, and as luck would have it, the guard was looking down the other one as he came into sight. Chuck's hands flew out in rapid succession and the two knives landed solidly, one in the chest and one in the neck. The entry gurgled slightly and fell backwards. Stu followed up with his bow, hitting first one guard and then the other, dropping both. None of the three had made enough of a sound to wake their companions, and the friends entered the room unchallenged.

Most of the archways had intricate drawings on them, all featuring stylized lizard people. The humidity made it difficult to tell how old the drawings were, but something within Allison told her that several were related to worship of whatever god the lizard folk venerated. She clenched her teeth at the sight at one of those particular ones having been smeared with sewer filth. While she knew that Chuck made a point of not angering deities purely for practical reasons, Allison's connection to her own Goddess made any sort of blasphemy seem especially bad.

There were three sets of bunks set up along the walls. Two of the sets were filled, and the third had just a single sleeping man in it. Set next to each of the beds was the occupants' equipment, all of which included a sword, shield, and shirt of mail. A makeshift platform had been built over the center of the room elevating the living space several inches above the muck. There were a mismatched set of table and chairs atop the platform, as well as several wooden stools, and a set of dice lay scattered across the table's surface. Quietly, the friends looked around the room for ropes that could be used to tie up those still sleeping. Once they had gathered enough, they moved into position. Chuck went to one bunk, drawing a dagger as he went. Stu nocked an arrow in his bow and made sure his quiver was free, so he could draw another if necessary. Jimmy placed himself in the center of the chamber, his sword out and ready, and TJ and Allison just hung back out of potential hand to hand combat.

When everyone was in place, Jimmy shouted, "OK,

everyone up, but if you do anything we don't like, you're dead."

All five bodies jerked up and began to roll out of bed but one by one they saw the friends ready to attack, giving them pause. Their companions' bodies on the floor only served to reinforce their caution. One of the guards raised his hands in surrender and said, "OK, OK. There's no need to get violent. We'll do whatever you want us to." He raised himself to a sitting position and when his companions saw he was not immediately attacked, they sat up as well.

"All of you, out of your beds slowly and move toward the center of the room. No sudden movements, no reaching for your weapons," Stu barked, bow aimed at the one who had spoken.

The leader stood up from his bed, hands still out, saying, "Oh, no worries. You have that bow pointed at us. We wouldn't do anything that might get us killed, would we, boys?"

There was a murmur of agreement from the others and all five stepped away from their bunks. "Good," said Jimmy. "Now sit down on the floor so we can tie you up. There's no need for this to get messy."

"Oh yes sir," came the reply. Suddenly, on some unseen command, the five dodged back to their bunks to grab their swords and shields. Quickly, Stu released his arrow, catching the leader in his back and the man fell to the ground lifeless. At the same time Chuck lunged forward with his dagger, the blade sliding in to the hilt. Stu drew and fired a second arrow, but his target had already taken hold of his shield and the missile bounced harmlessly off with a resounding clang. Jimmy let out a roar and charged toward where the two guards stood together, sword raised overhead.

The pair met him with shields raised, but the sheer power of his first swing knocked one to his knees. As Jimmy spun for the follow up the other guard stepped in front with his own shield, deflecting the blow and giving his companion the chance to regain his balance. Grunting in frustration, Jimmy redoubled his attack, slashing first left and then right, alternating between shields, trying to simply beat them into submission. Every so often one of them slipped the point of their swords towards him, and while most of the attacks were deflected by the shirt of mail he had received from the Bonecrushers, they managed to score several hits. While the berserker blood-lust allowed him to ignore the pain, each cut or nick sapped him of a little more strength and his breath became labored. Just as he began to worry he couldn't keep up the fight, he felt his body infused by new strength. Surprised, he looked around quickly and saw Allison, her eyes closed and her hand outstretched toward him.

An arrow flew past Jimmy to lodge itself in one of his opponent's knees and the man gave a cry of pain as his leg gave out. Seeing his chance, Jimmy lunged forward and drove his sword straight through the injured man. His target gave his sword a last, halfhearted, swing, but it was easily deflected by Jimmy's magical armor. Withdrawing his sword from his fallen foe, Jimmy squared off against the other guard.

TJ, for his part, was caught unawares by the sudden violence. He had relaxed when it seemed that their enemies were giving up without a fight, so rather than being able to conjure one of his large blasts of fire using reagents from his pouch, he had to settle for one of the weaker, targeted beams. The bolt of energy crashed into the upraised shield of Jimmy's remaining opponent, and rather than being deflected, the energy passed through the metal and the man staggered back. There were few who could stand against Jimmy one on one under the best of circumstances, and the large man quickly took advantage of the opportunity by beating the guard's shield away and giving him a deep slash across his torso.

After stabbing the first man, Chuck had crossed to where the leader's bunkmate stood ready to defend himself. Almost immediately the rogue found himself hard pressed. He had never been much of a fighter, and his dagger was no match for the sword and shield he faced, so he slowly gave ground, hoping for someone to provide him backup. As he did so he took a number of cuts across the arms and one stab to his shoulder. Stu sent several arrows in his direction, but the guard made deft use of his shield, blocking each shot in turn.

Out of the corner of her eye, Allison saw a glint of metal and she turned her head just in time to see a sword go into TJ's back and out his chest in a shower of blood. One of the sentries that Stu had first shot had stood up, the arrow still sticking out of his chest. The man winced in pain as he moved, but otherwise didn't seem particularly bothered by the wound. Quickly scanning the room, she saw the other man with an arrow in him standing up as well. "Guys! Things are starting to look bad," she called out, swinging her mace at the head of the guy who had just stabbed TJ.

"As opposed to how they were already looking?" Chuck shouted back, keeping his eyes on his opponent.

"Really bad!"

At the urgency in her voice, he gave a quick look and his eyes grew wide. "You have got to be kidding me," he muttered, continuing to back up, suddenly worried about not only the opponent in front of him but also being attacked from the side. The man he faced gave him an evil grin and leapt forward to press the attack. Knowing it was only a matter of time before he was brought down by fatigue and blood loss, Chuck charged to meet him. He threw himself toward the ground, rolling under the guard's slash and back up to his knees just behind the shield's protection. He jammed his dagger up and in and held it there until the sword and shield dropped to the ground.

The group's leader, as well as the one Chuck had dropped when they first lunged for their weapons pulled themselves back up from the ground. They looked shaky on their feet, but appeared to be getting stronger by the moment. Each drew their own weapons from the piles next to their bunks and entered the fray. It was now the four friends versus six apparently unkillable guards and both Jimmy and Chuck were clearly running close to the end of their energy. Their opponents, on the other hand, resumed their attacks with zeal and utter disregard for their own well-being. It appeared that knowing they couldn't die—or at least it was very hard for them to do so—gave them greater courage. Stu had been forced to drop his bow and draw his own sword to engage in melee, a clear last resort. Things appeared grim.

The sound of boots splashing in slop echoed down one of the tunnels and it took Chuck only a moment to realize that it wasn't the tunnel through which they had arrived. The sound didn't herald the cavalry coming to save the day —or at least not their cavalry. Surveying the scene, it didn't look like anyone was getting out of this alive. TJ was already down, and Stu had been forced to give up his most potent weapon for his least. Jimmy looked like he was beginning to tire, and Chuck knew his own abilities in a fight were less than stellar. Allison was, well, Allison. She wasn't built to fight, even with that smite spell she had taken. He, himself, had been wounded far too badly to make a run for it, as much as his instincts told him to.

In the few moments that no one was paying attention to him, he crouched behind the table and reached into one of the many pockets in his cloak to withdraw a specially prepared dagger. He slid the weapon from its sheath and inspected its blade closely, then with one fluid movement stood up and threw the dagger across the room. The blade left a thin slash across Allison's left arm, then clattered into the wall behind her. Chuck then charged forward at the nearest of the enemies, shouting at the top of his lungs.

The sound of marching boots grew louder and twenty men, all armed with bows, entered from one of the side tunnels. Leading the troop in a uniform with officer's plume was Winston, Hallowell's personal assistant. After only a moment's hesitation as he looked at the combatants he commanded, "Shoot the lot of them." Without question, the archers let loose arrow after arrow into the room, without regard for friend or foe, until there was no one left moving. He nodded his approval, 'Retrieve your arrows and let's get the lot of them moved back to headquarters. Tie the hands and feet of the newcomers. The boss'll tell us what to do about them when we get there." The men hurried to comply, pulling arrows out of bodies or unrolling stretchers on which to place the unconscious combatants. After a quick count of the bodies Winston amended, "There are too many. Stack the lighter ones together on a single stretcher. I only want to make one trip." He made a circuit of the room, stepping and frowning at the trail of sludge that the friends had tracked in. "I'm not sure how they found us down here, I'm glad we had those sentries posted."

One of the archers called over, "Sir? I think this one's actually dead."

Winston frowned at the man. "That's not possible. We all know we can't be killed down here. In fact, we've all experienced it, at least once."

The soldier bobbed his head. "Even so, sir, there's no breath, no heart, no nothing. I think the body's actually even begun to cool a bit."

Winston sighed and approached where the body lay. A quick inspection showed that it was, indeed, a corpse, and after he knelt down to take a closer look said, "Oh, but this is pretty, though," and slid a jeweled band from one of the body's fingers. Standing, he added, "Well that's odd. We'll need to let the boss know about that, too. I don't know about you, but if I might actually die for real the next time I have to fight, you can bet I'm going to be a bit more careful." He scanned the room, looking at the other bodies with arrow shafts sticking out of them. "Even so, it looks like it worked for everyone else, so maybe this was a fluke. Just leave the body here. If we roll it into the muck it could cause a blockage and we don't need another one of those, do we?" The men all nodded, remembering some prior refuse backup in the sewers. "Hopefully the rats will do the cleanup for us."

In short order the men were ready to leave, bodies carried on stretchers and bows over their shoulders. The group marched out in single file, leaving nothing but the furniture and Allison's body, laying gently in repose.

CHAPTER 20

A voice drifted out of the darkness. "Wake up. Can you hear me? Wake up!" Allison's eyes opened slowly. Her vision was blurry so she couldn't see who had propped her against a pillow and was pressing a cup of something to her hands. She groaned and the voice continued, "Here, drink thissss. It will make you feel better."

"Ik'tha'bor? Is that you? Where am I? What happened?" Her fingers wrapped around the cup and, with help, she brought it to her lips.

"I do not know, becaussse I was not here when it happened. But you are sssstill here where you and your friendssss fought. I am not sssstrong enough to carry you far, sssso I moved you onto one of their bedssss to wait with you. I hoped that you would wake up before they came back, becaussse I cannot fight. Can you walk?"

She wiggled her arms and legs and found that while she had suffered no permanent damage, she was extremely fatigued. Her healing power still smoldered within her, but she knew she could not rely on it yet. "No, but give me a few minutes and I should be able to stand up."

Her eyes cleared and when she focused on the lizard man, concern was clear in his reptilian features. "Can you remember anything that happened? Where are your friendssss?"

"I remember the fight was going well." She began slowly. "We had them beaten easily, but then they stood back up and started fighting us again." Her voice choked up as she relived seeing a sword driven through her best friend. "We should have known this would happen, but somehow we just forgot about it. The people we were fighting, they showed no fear whatsoever, because they knew that we couldn't kill them after all. And then there was the arrow in my chest and I started to black out. Except that I didn't quite black out completely." She paused a moment. "They said I was dead. I remember that. They carried everyone else off to go get healed, but they left me here because they thought I was dead. How could I have been dead? And how did you know I wasn't?"

"You did not ssssmell dead. That issss how I knew. You looked dead, and felt dead, but did not ssssmell dead." She gave a silent prayer of thanks that he hadn't said she didn't tassssste dead, then immediately felt guilty at the thought. He continued. "I do not know the anssssswerssss to thosssse other quesssstionssss, but I do know that we cannot sssstay here. As ssssoon as you are able to move, we need to go. It hassss only been two hourssss since you came into the ssssewerssss, and they are not far away, and could come back at any time. Esssspecially if they fear another attack, they will come with more men. We musssst go if you can."

"OK, OK," she groaned. "I'll see what I can do." She reached into herself and was pleased to find that the power had already grown from just minutes before. She let the healing wash through her, and much of the fatigue she felt disappeared, though her joints still felt stiff and there was a sharp pain where the arrow had pierced her breastplate. She reached up and was surprised to find the it still protruding from her chest. "Well that explain the pain, I guess." She considered for a moment. "We're going to have to leave it in for now. Pulling it out will cause more damage than I can heal right now, and at least the wound has closed so I won't bleed to death. Let's go."

She lowered her feet over the side of the bunk, and with Ik'tha'bor's help, she stood up on wobbly legs. The pain in her chest was intense, but she bit down and bore it. They didn't have time for her to build up the healing power it would take to patch herself up. She channeled what was left of her power into her knees to bolster their failing strength, and then, with one arm draped over the lizard man's shoulder, slowly began to walk. She could only take a few steps at a time before stopping for breath, but with his help they left the battle site and began the long walk back to the surface.

As they walked, and as she felt her power rekindle, she continued to cast minor healing spells on herself so that by the time they arrived back at the alleyway she no longer had to rely on Ik'tha'bor's help. Her spirit, though, had been crushed. Her friends were down there, and she was up here, and there wasn't a single thing she could do about it. She sat down in the rain and cried.

From out of the darkness came a voice. "Well, look what we have here..."

CHAPTER 21

The voice was quiet and not unkind, and a glimmer of light from behind a stack of crates broke the darkness. Ik'tha'bor hissed and looked around frantically for an avenue of escape. Finding none, he began to pull Allison back down into the sewer. She firmly, but gently, resisted his tugs. "No, I know that voice. I think he's a friend."

"As good a friend as you are likely to find in this gods-forsaken place. I feel dirty just being here." A figure stepped into view, the torch held above his head hissing in the downpour. Edmond, the warlord's son, stood in front of her, wearing a full suit of chain armor and armed to the teeth. "Unless I miss my guess, you look like you could use a little help." His handsome grin faltered slightly at the sight of Ik'tha'bor's bared teeth, and fell completely when his eyes fell on the arrow protruding from her armor.

Allison gave him a pained look. "Yes, but I doubt you can give me that help. At least, not unless you brought an army with you. There were too many of them for the five of us, and I'm the only one that got out. I still don't know how. If we went back in there, they would simply capture you as well."

"Well first things first," he replied. "In case you didn't notice, you have got an arrow sticking out of your chest, and I'm sure that can't be comfortable. Though I commend you on your ability to withstand pain, we need to get that out of you." He drew a knife as he approached her, ignoring the angry hiss coming from the lizard man. With one deft cut he sliced through the arrow flush with her armor. "With your permission?" He asked, then released the clasps beneath each armpit that held her breastplate together. Edmund gently removed the armor's front so that he had access to the remaining nub of arrow protruding from her padded gambeson. Another man approached, face covered in tattoos and holding a small fetish doll in his hand. At her inquiring glance, Edmund explained, "Healer." He gripped the arrow tightly and looked her in the eyes. "Ready?" She nodded and he yanked as hard as he could.

When she regained consciousness several minutes later Allison found her chest bound tightly in a bandage, a crimson spot where the arrow had been. Edmund offered her a small canteen. "Here, drink this. It will dull the pain a bit."

"You should have given it to me *before* you did that," she grumbled and took a long gulp of the liquid. Fire shot down her throat and she coughed violently. Sputtering, she asked, "What *was* that? Are you trying to help me or kill me?"

Edmund only laughed and put the bottle to his own

lips for a swig. "This is the good stuff. Whiskey straight from my father's private stash." He tucked the bottle back into a pouch then said, "Come on. We need to get you out of this cold and rain." He reached to help her up, but she swatted away his hand.

"No, we don't need to get me anywhere. We have to figure out a way to get my friends back and get your artifact back and get Lord Hallowell back and get Ik'tha'bor his home back. That's what we need to do, and to hell with your cold and rain." She paused a moment or two and then said a little softer. "Whoa, you're right. That IS the good stuff. Can I get another sip?"

He chuckled but shook his head and replied, "No, I think you've had plenty, and you are absolutely right about all the other stuff. I just wanted to hear it from you directly. You want to know what army I brought with me?" He gave a whistle and another armored figure—she immediately recognized her as the one who had nearly killed her combatant in the Challenge—stepped forward and said with a salute, "Yes, Lord?"

"Pass the word, Captain. We're headed in."

Edmund assisted Allison in putting her breastplate back on, then led her back out of the alleyway. She was pleased and surprised to discover that there were close to three hundred men and women, a mix of traditionalists wearing leather armor and ones armored like Edmund in the more modern chain. Even more surprising was the fact that there were several dozen men and women with bows slung over their shoulders. When she asked, Edmund said that while it may not be the bravest method of fighting, it was definitely effective, and in these days giving up an obvious advantage like that would be akin to fighting without armor.

"How did you get all those people past the guards? Surely they didn't just let this many armed soldiers walk into the city, did they?"

"Actually, yes they did. It seems that the watch is all up in arms about things, and while on average the members of the Watch here are city-dwelling, wall-hiding cowards, there were some who saw beyond their standard orders and decided to be useful." He pulled out a piece of paper and held it out to her. "This note you sent didn't hurt either. When the gate guard saw that you were planning on rescuing his commander, and when we told him that we were coming to help, he let us pass right on through. Even sent an escort with us so that we would get to the right place, though even with their help this was the fifth alley I checked before finding you."

"So, what's the plan?"

"I was sort of hoping you folks would have one. This isn't our turf. From what I can tell, you had one, but it didn't work so well."

"Well I think the plan itself wasn't so bad. We caught the first batch by surprise and should have had them subdued easily. What we didn't count on was the fact that they didn't stay dead. Oh, and the reinforcements with bows didn't help either." She ruefully fingered the hole in her breastplate.

Edmund smiled. "Well this time you're the one with

reinforcements. I can't imagine that we won't outnumber them, so if it means we simply overwhelm them and sit on their heads until they give up, then that'll be what we do."

The captain cleared her throat and said, "But sir, what about…?"

Edmund waived away the protest. "Oh, don't trouble her about that, Tilly. Just make sure the men are prepared and ready to go."

"Yes, sir. We are ready, sir."

"Well then let's get moving. But there is one thing." He turned to Allison. "You stay back, understood? You have been through too much today already, and you are only going to get in the way." She looked away until he took her by the chin and turned her face to his. "Do you promise? Because if you don't, you're staying up here and that's that."

"No," was her response.

"I'm sorry?" He looked confused.

"You heard me," she asserted, pulling herself to her full height. "As you said, the city isn't your turf, and not only are those *my* friends trapped down there, it's *my* friend who knows how to lead you there." She put her hand on Ik'tha'bor's shoulder. "Either I'm in the front with you, or your precious battle standard can rot down there." She didn't have to mention the fact that the permanent loss of the artifact would mean his father's tenure as warlord would come to a quick, violent, end.

He held her eyes for a few moments longer, then nodded. "Fine." He turned to Ik'tha'bor. The lizard man was twiddling his fingers anxiously as he gazed at the large quantity of armed men. "I don't suppose I could ask a favor of you?"

Ik'tha'bor looked to Allison for guidance, and when she nodded her head encouragingly said, "Me? What do you want me to do, ssssir?" His eyes started shifting about nervously, looking for a way to bolt.

"Is there another way down to where your home is other than the one here in this alley? There won't be any advantage in numbers if we're all coming from the same way and only the first ten or so can fight."

"Yessss, there are other wayssss in. Many wayssss."

"Could you take me along with some of my men to another of these ways and lead us to your home?"

The lizard man stood frozen for a few moments as he thought through the alternatives. Finally, he nodded and said, "Yessss, I will do thissss."

"Are you sure?" asked Allison. "You have done so much already, including saving my life."

"Yessss. You and your friends rissssked themsssselvessss for me and my family. It issss the leasssst I can do." After a moment he added, "And if we want to get our home back, the invaderssss need to be ssssent away."

Edmund ended the conversation. "Then it's settled. Allison will show Tilly and half the group back down this path, and our new friend will take me and the others. If we leave now, can we all be there at the same time, or should we delay?"

"Yessss, there is a shorter path that issss more direct. I will take your men there, and if Allisssson moves at a normal walking paccccce, we will arrive at the sssame time."

"OK, then let's go." He quickly split his followers into two groups, placing all the archers under Tilly's command. He extended a hand to Allison. "Good luck, Lady. Spirits protect you."

"And may the Goddess watch over you," she replied, making a quick sign of reverence she didn't know she knew. She returned to the alley and descended the steps into the darkness.

The People carried torches instead of lanterns so that in a battle they could drop their lights wherever they were standing. The downside was that the torches gave off a thick black smoke that accumulated about their heads within the enclosed sewers. Allison directed half of them to douse their flames and she was pleased to discover that the group followed her order immediately. Now that she knew the way, it was a much quicker trip. Allison was amazed at how little noise the group made as they marched, despite its numbers. In spite of her magical boots, she was still the loudest of the group. Like Chuck earlier, some jumped to the other side so that the line was only half as long.

When they arrived at the site of the earlier battle they found it deserted. Allison stopped for a moment to remember which tunnel the archers had come from, then pointed said, "This way." Another five minutes' travel brought them to more torchlight. Across the sewer had been built a low wall that effectively blocked the muck from going any further in this direction. That would keep the smell—or at least the mess—out of the main living areas. With no muck in the central channel, the men and women accompanying Allison spread out across the entire width as they moved the last hundred feet.

There was a sentry standing at the end of tunnel, though, luckily, he had his back to them. Tilly gave a hand signal and one of the tenters darted forward. He put one arm around the sentry's neck and his other on his mouth, and dragged him back to where the rest were waiting. A burly woman gave him a whack with a club on the back of his head, knocking him unconscious. The group crept closer until they could see into the large chamber at the tunnel's end. They were roughly halfway up the wall, which gave them an unobstructed view of the entire area. The chamber was enormous—easily the size of a football field, and small platforms had been built into the walls overlooking the central arena. Well-dressed men and women filled the platforms, many looking eagerly toward the center of the room. On the centermost platform, talking to a man decked out in jewelry and furs, stood another, fur-clad man who gave off an aura of importance and command. It took Allison a moment to place where she'd seen him before and then it clicked. Winston. The castellan's right-hand man. As she watched, it seemed to Allison that he was the one behind the whole scheme. As she watched, the pair broke into laughs and she felt a knot twist in her stomach.

It became clear why the sentry had been facing inward rather than out—they had arrived just in time to see the beginning of one of the gladiatorial events. On one side of the arena floor was a large cage containing a creature that looked to Allison like a cross between a tiger and a rhinoceros. On the other side were several human figures, one of whom she thought was Count Hallowell.

The men were dressed in poor quality armor and the

weapons they held looked as if they had been pulled out of the sewer and handed directly to the combatants. It didn't look like a fair fight at all. Around the edge of the arena were soldiers dressed similarly to those whom she and her friends had fought earlier. Some had bows, but most had shields and long spears. From the looks of things, the spearmen were there to keep the gladiators from trying to escape, and the archers were there to spur them along in case they didn't feel like fighting.

"Archers forward," hissed Allison and the full company of men approached the tunnel entrance with their bows strung and arrows at hand. As they moved into position a flash of movement across the expanse indicated another sentry had also been subdued. Tilly smiled and said, "Your friend's timing is excellent. How do you want to do this? We could take out the lot of them with arrows now or give them a chance to surrender."

Allison was taken aback at the question. As much as she had wanted to be in charge, she hadn't expected to have to make that sort of a decision. "Um," she began, stalling for time. A quick count revealed there were fewer than a hundred fighters in the room, including the gladiators. Those, she guessed, wouldn't be interested in fighting their rescuers, leaving perhaps seventy or eighty who might resist the tenter's attack. The choice of giving up or slaughter wasn't a bluff—either the kidnappers would surrender or it would be a bloodbath as Tilly's troops rained arrows down on them from above and Edmund cleaned up stragglers. "I think we should give them the chance. Besides, we don't know who down there is really on the other side, and who were kidnapped to provide their entertainment. Even if they wouldn't actually die, I'd rather avoid them the agony of getting turned into pincushions."

A flash of something showed in Tilly's face for the briefest moment before she replied, "Fair enough. Some of ours are down there, too." She looked to where her men were waiting. "Get ready, folks. It's about to get messy." She gave Allison a nod.

Allison stepped to the lip of the tunnel, and shouted, "Attention! You are surrounded, and there is no chance of escape." Her voice boomed unnaturally, as if her magic knew she was addressing a crowd, almost like a temple sermon. "If you all put down your weapons you will be taken into custody and turned over to the Watch. If you don't, then it will get messy, and then you'll be turned over to the watch."

From the other side she heard Edmund shout, "If you don't," he paused slightly, "you will all die where you stand." Allison turned to Tilly, who shrugged.

There was a rustling of weapons and all the well-dressed men and women on the platforms started talking all at once and pointing. "Oh really?" The man standing next to Winston called back. He raised a hand to his brow and pretended to squint. "I see a few dozen men, and we have easily three times as many. Plus, in case you hadn't heard, no one here can die. Which means that when we have defeated you and your pathetic rabble you will join the ranks of those who fight for our amusement. What do you think of that?" The assembled gallery let out a laugh.

"Well this is what I think of that. Anyone who puts

down their weapons will be spared. Everyone else…" she gave an exaggerated shrug.

"So you say." He waved his hand dismissively and then muttered something to Winston, who hopped down from the platform onto the lower level.

"Attack!" He shouted and charged around the edge of the arena, gathering his soldiers as he went.

"So be it," murmured Tilly. "Fire at will." Arrows flew through the air targeting the enemy archers. Several arrows flew back toward them, but a shield wall was quickly erected and the missiles bounced harmlessly off. When the last of the archers around the arena had been toppled, Tilly said, "Two volleys to the sides, then retire. Again arrows flew, but rather than targeting the charging spearmen, they were directed into the galleries where the spectators were still watching with amused looks on their faces. The mirth quickly changed to horror as nobles expecting an evening of entertainment found themselves to be targets. Cries of pain echoed across the chamber, and Tilly said only loud enough for Allison to hear, "We gave them a choice."

As commanded, the archers backed up, leaving tenters with sword and shield to meet the onrushing spearmen. The higher ground afforded them some protection from the spears' longer reach, but even so the combat quickly became bloody. More than once Allison ran to one of the fallen to stabilize their wounds with a burst of magic. She'd then motion for a comrade to drag the wounded out of harm's reach, their places taken by a fresh warrior. The soldiers below suffered losses as well, though their injured were treated with a cold, professional indifference. After several minutes of back and forth, it became clear that the two groups were fighting to something of a stalemate. Neither side was able to press the advantage, and it looked to be simply a question of which group wore itself out sooner.

Of course, it had never been the tenter's plan to fight that battle to anything other than a stalemate. In the chaos and noise none of the conspirators noticed their second force pouring out of the other sewer tunnel. The newcomers closed the distance between them and the spearmen at a run, catching the spearmen completely unawares. The guards' shields faced where Allison's soldiers stood, so they were unprotected from the swords that crashed down upon them. A quarter of the spearmen fell in the first few seconds, including those with officer's plumes on their helmets, and by the time the others realized that they had been outflanked they were too disorganized to reform their shield walls to protect their rear. The melee was over in minutes, with all of the enemies and perhaps twenty of the People lying bleeding on the ground. Mystics stepped forward from the backs of the tunnels to heal the wounded, and Allison joined them to help as much as she her limited powers permitted. Moans of pain came from the platforms around the sides of the arena, where the wounded called out for assistance.

Edmund approached her, smiling grimly at the scene. She asked, "Should we start tying up hands and feet now? They aren't out for long before they revive from the magic, right?"

He shook his head. "Not this time. They won't be

getting up from this fight. I meant what I said when I told them their choice was surrender or die."

"What do you mean?" she asked, confusion on her face. Her eyes found Tilly's face, though the other woman conspicuously avoided meeting Allison's gaze.

"One of the downsides to combat under the protection of the artifact is overconfidence. You described it earlier—men unafraid to die will take risks that they otherwise would not. I have seen many fights like that, where the two swung at each other recklessly, hoping for a lucky strike and not caring about defending themselves. That was our advantage here tonight. You see, those who created the artifact knew that sometimes we really did need to fight to kill. And of course, challenges for the warlord position had to be to the death. So, there is a ritual—a simple one, I am told—that deactivates the artifact. As soon as we came in sight of the arena, some of the mystics in my group performed it. So, while they fought with recklessness and fearlessness, we were cautious and made the best of our opportunities. As you see, we won.

"And now, to finish the job. You may not want to watch this." He drew his sword and motioned a number of his men forward. Together they entered the larger chamber and headed toward the nearest platform. There, several well-dressed spectators stood paralyzed with fear and several others lay wounded or dead. He climbed the ramp leading up and brought his sword around to strike.

"HOLD!" a voice commanded from the floor. Edmund turned his head at the sound, his sword poised to strike. "Those here who are still alive will be spared," the voice boomed up. Lord Hallowell strode toward them from the center of the chamber, his own sword raised. The older man looked battered and bruised, but despite the poor quality of his attire maintained an aura of nobility. "This is still my city, by the gods, and I am still in charge of its defense. There will be no more bloodshed tonight."

Edmund looked back and forth between the castellan and the noble cowering at his feet. The man's fine robes had been spattered with blood, and he held his arms protectively in front of his face. At last, Edmund lowered his weapon and ordered his men to do the same. "Were it any other man in this city asking me this, I would not have stayed my hand. But because of your influence here, and because you yourself have suffered at their hands, I will spare their lives."

Hallowell smiled. "Good choice, son. You've got a good head on your shoulders." The castellan approached the younger man and extended his hand, which Edmund took. "I think that this may turn into quite a pleasant relationship." He surveyed the bloody scene and called out, "Now let's get these people rounded up, find the rest of the captives and get out of here. If I never smell a sewer again it will be entirely too soon."

Allison agreed.

CHAPTER 22

After the battle, Edmund's men found all those who had been kidnapped, including Allison's friends, and returned them to the surface. They even managed to subdue the tiger-rhinoceros thing to be released in the forest. Most surprising to Allison about the whole thing was the discovery of her ring on Winston's finger. She hadn't realized it was gone, but had become so used to taking command of situations she didn't even think of needing to rely on it. Although if she'd known she had lost it, she might not have tried to order Edmund and his followers around; she figured his "character" was probably too strong to be swayed by its powers anyway. Perhaps, she thought, Jimmy was right, and she really was growing into her character as a temple priestess.

The five friends, now fully recovered from their injuries, were in a large reception hall, as were Edmund, his father, and a squad of Watch soldiers. Trays of meat and cheese sat atop every flat surface and several servants stood nearby with jugs of wine to refill any goblets that went empty. "Not a bad couple day's work, huh?" Hallowell said from his seat behind a large table desk before popping a cherry tomato into his mouth. Alfred, the young officer who had led the five from the dungeon just a few days before stood behind the castellan. His helmet had a different colored plume than it had before, indicating a recent promotion, and the man seemed to be taking his new responsibility seriously: his eyes darted about left and right as if expecting an assassin's blade to strike at any moment

"Well let's see," summarized Allison, ticking off her fingers as she spoke. "We stopped an underground gladiatorial ring, rooted out a chunk of corrupt nobles, exposed a spy in the Watch, and brought the city folk and the tent folk together. I'd say that really was a pretty solid effort, even if it did get a little harrowing from time to time."

"I'll say," said TJ, nervously rubbing a spot on his chest. His robe had been replaced from the government's vast stores, yet he kept fingering the place where his old one had been cut open. "I don't remember much, but that sword through my back wasn't very comfortable. It's a good thing the artifact hadn't been deactivated yet." The others nodded their agreement.

"And of course my promotion from castellan to lord protector," Hallowell concluded. "Regretfully, the prior holder of that office took an arrow in the neck in the battle, and many of his political bloc were among the other dead and wounded." The look on his face was anything but regretful. "When the council met in emergency session, I was the natural choice to be the city's new leader. I'll be moving to a new office later this week, once it's emptied out." He looked around the large room, easily ten times the size of his old office, before adding, "I do kind of like this one though, especially the windows. Maybe I'll just stay here. What do you think, Alfred?"

Startled, the officer stammered, "Easily defensible, sir, with access to at least three routes out of the castle in case we need to flee." Hallowell nodded his head and raised his hands in a "there you have it" motion.

"Almost as if you planned it, huh?" Chuck smirked and raised his goblet in a toast before taking a large gulp of wine.

"Oh, no, I'm neither that clever nor that self-sacrificing," their host shook his head. "If I had planned it, it would have been *you* that got kidnapped, not me." He grinned and raised his own cup to return the toast. "Or maybe that little weasel Winston. His being in on it all along certainly makes sense in retrospect. That probably explains why Stu was targeted as soon as you arrived in town. He probably hoped that the attempted kidnapping would convince you to flee instead of staying to investigate. He was also in on the fact that that we had no real case against you, so if you took off there'd be nothing stopping you."

"What now?" Stu asked. "Are we done here? I've had more than enough of this city."

"Well, there are a couple things that need to be addressed. The first is the fact that my former position is vacant and needs to be filled. I am not going to have the time to devote to running the police and the rest of the government together." He looked toward Edmund. "This is part of the reason why I asked you and the warlord to join us today. In light of your tremendous service to me and the city in general, at great potential risk to yourselves, I would like to offer the job to you." The two tenters looked at each other in surprise, and Hallowell continued. "I know that you are nomads and that this is perhaps only a temporary spot for you. That doesn't bother me. If you only fill it for six months or a year, that's fine. What I need now, most of all, is someone I can trust in that position, and you have earned that trust. You don't have to give me your answer now, but I will need one before the end of the week."

He turned to the warlord then continued. "Second, I would like the first act of my new administration to be to formalize the relationship between our two peoples. The mistrust with which we look at each other is unnecessary and unhelpful, particularly given the current environment. If we cannot work together, neither of us will be able to stand against the onslaught that is heading our way."

Edmund's father looked thoughtful, and was about to speak, but Allison interrupted. "The onslaught? I thought that Providence City was going to side with the Arcanum. At least that's what Thaddeus said you were planning on doing."

"That's what the *old* government planned to do. It turns out most of those in the camp in favor of allying with that mad wizard were part of the conspiracy. Suffice to say those who manage to keep their heads—and many will not

—will certainly not be keeping their positions within the government. As I indicated in my letter, I am very much in favor of your quest to stop the wizard's march westward. Providence City will not give up easily. And that brings me to the third point of this meeting.

"There is nothing material that I can offer you. I am sure that you know just how rich those gems you're carrying make you. Or at least one of you knows." He smiled at Chuck, who shrugged. "So, I can't very well pay you. Nor do I have any items of power that I can give to you to aid in your quest. I personally own none, and even if the city had any in the armory, I would not have the authority to gift them away. I can, however, do this. Every sword, shield and bow of our city are pledged to your cause. You have done us an immeasurable service at great risk to yourselves, showing us clearly on which side virtue lies. To a man, we will stand and fight and die beside you." He stood up and saluted them, clenched fist over heart. The soldiers in the room all snapped to attention and copied the salute.

TJ opened his mouth to speak but the warlord cut him off. "We, too, owe you a great deal. Not only did you help us to retrieve our most precious historical artifact, but you reunited us with those who were kidnapped and enslaved. We, the People, give you this oath as well. The upcoming fight may not be won by arms alone, but you shall not lack for them on account of us."

The friends stood dumbfounded. In less than a week they had gained the support of at least ten thousand battle-ready soldiers and, if Providence City's allies in the surrounding areas threw in with them, many thousands more. All of a sudden, the job they had set out to do looked manageable. Or at least more manageable. Like maybe even a job they could accomplish.

Jimmy took a bite from the turkey leg in his hand. “Not a bad couple days’ work, indeed.”

EPILOGUE

Again, the emissary stood in front of the wizard, the smugness he'd worn on his face during his prior visit long gone. The hat was no longer in evidence, and his previously well-maintained riding leathers looked as if he had slept under a hedge while wearing them. The man's whiskers had sprouted stubble all along his cheeks, giving his previously shapely beard a mangy appearance. The man himself may have been the same, but the person standing in front of the ornate throne was entirely different.

"Oh Greatness," the man began but Magnus cut him off.

"Spare me the pleasantries. You have news from your home, do you not?"

The emissary visibly swallowed, then nodded. "Yes, majesty. Conditions have…deteriorated since last we spoke. Control of the city has changed hands, and the ones who now have superiority are not as sympathetic to your cause as in the past."

"And how did this turn of affairs occur?" Magnus asked sweetly. He had long since learned what had happened through his own magical scrying, but enjoyed toying with the formerly pompous noble.

"We are not sure, oh Greatness. But many of our leaders—and my friends—were slain, devastating our bloc and catapulting the other into ascendency."

Magnus steepled his fingers together and placed them under his chin. "This wouldn't have anything to do with our last meeting, would it? When I gave you the ability to re-solidify your hold?" The man on the floor below him shuffled his feet uneasily. "Perhaps something to do with the greed of your leaders—and friends, as you mentioned—who, rather than destroying the object of power, decided to use it for their own enrichment and entertainment?" Now the man began looking around furtively for a manner of escape. "Or even a small band of meddling newcomers who, rather than being subdued and killed outright were given the opportunity to collapse your plans around your head?"

Magnus waved a hand in frustration. "This should all have been predictable, and I apologize to you for not identifying this outcome earlier."

The dusty man's eyebrows raise slightly in hope that even though he had been caught in a lie he might escape the worst punishment for it.

"I should have known that left to their own devices, your city's leaders would have concocted that ridiculous plan. I should have known that they would underestimate that groups abilities to figure out the scheme and disrupt it. I should have known that when all was said and done, a new regime, hostile to me, would be established. It was, after all, almost inevitable." Magnus's voice drifted off at the end, and his eyes wandered aimlessly about the room. When they refocused on the trembling man in front of him, he said again, "I apologize. This was out of your control this entire time. You are dismissed."

Without hesitation, the man turned and bolted from the room. His home was no longer safe, but he had assets squirreled away in other cities and could start anew. At least he had his life.

Magnus sat for several long minutes before raising his voice. "Captain…" The emissary had served him well.

ACKNOWLEDGMENTS

I would like to express my deepest gratitude for all those who have encouraged me to continue to write, not least of all my family, who are extraordinarily tolerant of my ignoring dishes, laundry and other staples of modern household life while I am writing. I continue to be surprised when people ask me how when book two is coming out, especially James from Totalcon, for whom that is always the second question after "How are you?" My beta readers, Andrew, Christopher, Danielle, Natalie, Paul, and Pip gave me great ideas about how to make the story better. Then, Jenn, Sandra, Sara (my hero!) and Sarah took on the herculean effort of finding typos. I really appreciate all that work. All remaining errors are entirely mine.

When I asked Karen Lucky to do my cover, I never imagined it would turn out as wonderfully as it did. Thank you.

Lastly, I continue to owe a debt of gratitude to Adam,

Dan, Rachel and Rachel from Legendary/Nerdist for taking a shot on me in the first place, and for the folks at Inkshares for welcoming me so warmly to book publishing. You folks are all pretty awesome.

ABOUT THE AUTHOR

Dave Barrett lives with his wife, three children, and an active imagination in Hampden, Maine, where he teaches financial accounting at the University of Maine. His first novel, *It's All Fun and Games*, was selected as a winner of the inaugural Nerdist Collection Contest.

CPSIA information can be obtained
at www.ICGtesting.com
Printed in the USA
LVHW031546060619
620404LV00036B/874

9 780578 214610